Book 2

THE UNHINGED SERIES

More by Nicole Edwards

The Alluring Indulgence Series
Kaleb
Zane
Travis
Holidays with the Walker Brothers
Ethan
Braydon
Sawyer
Brendon

The Club Destiny Series
Conviction
Temptation
Addicted
Seduction
Infatuation
Captivated
Devotion
Perception
Entrusted

The Dead Heat Ranch Series
Boots Optional
Betting on Grace

The Devil's Bend Series
Chasing Dreams
Vanishing Dreams

Standalone Novels
A Million Tiny Pieces

Writing as Timberlyn Scott
Unhinged
Unraveling
Chaos

Unraveling

BOOK 2
The Unhinged Series

Nicole Edwards

Writing as **Timberlyn Scott**

SL Independent Publishing, LLC
PO Box 806
Hutto, Texas 78634
www.slipublishing.com

Unraveling, Book 2 – **An Unhinged Novel** is a work of fiction. Names, characters, businesses, places, events and incidents either are the products of the author's imagination or used in a fictitious manner. Any resemblance to actual persons, living or dead, business establishments, events, or locales is entirely coincidental.

Cover Image: © Artem Furman - Fotolia.com
Cover Design: © Nicole Edwards Limited
Editing: Blue Otter Editing

ISBN: 978-1-939786-33-3

Dedication

This book is dedicated to:

My daughter.

To have you in my cheering section
means more to me than you will ever know.

Contents

Chapter One

Sebastian

Saturday night

I'll be the first to admit that I wasn't sure how things went south so quickly, but one minute Payton was lying in my arms and I was mustering up the strength to tell her who I was. And then bam! In walked Aaron, slamming shit around in the other room, and Payton was gone.

As much as I wanted to say I was disappointed, the truth was … I wasn't.

My nerves were shot, there was no doubt about that, but the guy's timing couldn't have been better, to be honest. There could've been plenty of other times when Aaron's volatile arrival would've put a damper on things that might have been going on between Payton and me in her bedroom, but not today.

Didn't matter that I had no idea why Aaron was there in the first place.

Regardless, he had actually just saved the day as far as I was concerned. I had almost spilled my guts to a woman I was hoping to hang on to for longer than a fucking minute. Damn near spewed the thoughts that I had never spoken to anyone before. Not Leif, not Toby. No one. The secret that I've kept locked up inside me was one that would change the life of many, and not in a good way, either. So Aaron's interruption was welcome.

As it was, I had informed Payton that I was related to her boss, although I had done so without giving her the disturbing details. Telling her that I was Conrad Trovato's son hadn't freaked her out, which I was a tad surprised by, but I also considered that a good thing. But the earth-shattering revelation that had nearly followed likely would have. Okay, there really was no "likely" about it, she would have freaked.

But I hadn't shared my deepest, darkest secret, and here I was, following Payton into the small living room of her apartment while she yelled at her friend Aaron and he yelled back.

"What the hell is going on?" Chloe shouted when she joined the rest of us in the living room dressed in some sort of form-fitting pink yoga pants and a black T-shirt, her hair wet and dripping down her back.

And now there were three.

I laughed. I couldn't help myself. Everyone was yelling, but the only thing they seemed to be saying was "Why is everyone yelling?"

Counterproductive if you asked me.

But no one did because … well, because they were too busy shouting at one another.

I glanced over at the tall blond guy who'd accompanied Payton to Conrad's party last week to see him standing in the kitchen, his head hanging down, palms planted firmly on the counter. His muscles were tense, the skin on his face pulled tautly, and if I wasn't mistaken, he was shaking.

He looked pissed, but then again, that could have been his happy face.

I didn't know the guy.

"What's wrong?" Payton asked Aaron again, her voice significantly lower.

"Mark."

That was the only word that Aaron said, yet Chloe and Payton both nearly crumbled as they ran to Aaron's side, throwing their arms around him.

I fought the growl that rumbled deep in my chest. Watching Payton put her arms around another man wasn't something I would ever enjoy seeing, I realized right then. Clearly she cared for this guy, but to watch her hugging him went miles past my comfort zone. Instead of interrupting, I leaned against the doorjamb and continued to observe quietly.

"What did he do, honey?" Chloe asked Aaron, her wide green eyes intently focused on him.

"The bastard cheated on me," Aaron grumbled.

Ahh. So it went like that, did it?

Hug away, Payton. Hug away.

Could I say that I was happy that this Aaron guy was pissed off? It wasn't all that enjoyable to watch, so no. However, finding out the guy was gay pretty much made my whole fucking day. And at this point, after the fight I'd had with my father earlier, I'd had a pretty shitty day.

Aaron was gay.

You're probably asking how I know his sexual preference based on his reaction. Well, it all made sense now, and it really didn't have anything to do with his outburst. First off, any guy would have to be gay not to look at Payton with lust in his eyes, and aside from a severe possessive expression when he'd approached us on the veranda the night of Conrad's party, Aaron hadn't looked at her like he was ready to toss her on the bed and have his wicked way with her. That had been one of the first things I'd noticed that night. And hell, even my two best friends had shared their desire to "do her," although I'd been ready to string them up by the balls at the time. Second, the guy's hair was too fucking perfect, as were his clothes. I mean, seriously, he had an emblem on his navy blue polo. Dude had to be gay.

Sure, I guess it was possible that this "Mark" person was really Markanne or Markella, but I highly doubted it. After all, the guy was a bastard, according to Aaron.

"I'll go over there and punch him in the nose," Payton offered Aaron, her tone sympathetic.

Damn. And now she was threatening physical violence. My dick was instantly hard again. Fan-fucking-tastic. Such a sweet face, so innocent and pure, was threatening to punch some asshole in the face. I think I fell in love with her right then.

Aaron turned his head slightly to the left to look at Payton. From where I stood, I could see a small smile tilting his lips.

"You wanna talk about it?" Payton asked him, and that was the moment Aaron must have noticed I was standing there, because he looked up, his tired blue eyes meeting mine.

He wasn't smiling anymore.

"What the hell are you doing here?" he asked me directly.

I smirked. I had no idea what the hell to say to that.

Payton smacked him in the arm. "Don't be rude."

"Sorry," Aaron replied, but I knew he wasn't apologizing to me. The guy was protective of Payton. That was obvious.

Again, I couldn't say that his brotherly response to Payton bothered me.

Although I didn't need help in the protective department, it didn't hurt that someone had her best interest in mind. As long as he and I could get along, we'd do fine.

"Fuck him," I stated firmly. "This Mark guy, that is," I explained as I continued. "You don't need that cheating bastard."

All eyes turned to me, a little dazed and a lot confused. I fought the urge to laugh again. These three amused me.

"What?" I pushed off the wall and took two steps into the small living room.

A knock on the front door pulled me up short. We all glanced over, but no one made a move to answer. I turned back to Payton and cocked an eyebrow. She nodded, and I made my way to the door, gripping the knob and pulling it open.

"Hey, dude. What's up?" Toby greeted me with a cheesy-ass grin.

With a smile of my own, I closed the door in his face and turned back to the others.

Aaron laughed, Payton smirked, and Chloe glared at me.

What did she expect?

"Let him in," Chloe instructed, her hands on her hips, head tilted to the side as if she couldn't figure me out.

No one could. I liked to think that was part of my charm. "He's a big boy. He knows how to open a door," I told her before dropping onto the couch to watch the show.

And just like I'd predicted, Toby turned the knob and walked into the apartment, still grinning from ear to ear.

A couple of good things about Toby: he didn't get his feelings hurt easily and he rarely ever held a grudge. Hell, it wasn't often that I even saw the guy in a bad mood.

"No one mentioned there was a party," Toby said, looking from one person to another, his gaze stopping on me.

"No party. We're consoling the gay guy," I offered, propping my ankle on my knee and leaning back on the couch. Nodding in Aaron's direction, I added, "His douche of a boyfriend cheated."

"No way," Toby said, pretending to be serious. "Dude, you don't need that shit. I say fuck that loser."

"Not a good idea," I said in a mock whisper, looking directly at Toby. "The fucker's already got that covered."

"Oh. Right," Toby stated, his fist resting beneath his chin, his index finger tapping on his lips as though he was thinking. "String him up by his balls. It's the only way to fix it."

I glanced over at the three still in the kitchen, waiting to see what they'd say to Toby's words of wisdom.

And just like that, everyone was laughing.

That was what I loved about Toby. He didn't take anything seriously. Well, most things, anyway. There was a time and place for everything, and Toby was mature enough to know that, but for the most part, he was a laid-back, good ol' boy with a wicked sense of humor. And since I wasn't all that fond of confrontation thanks to the constant battles I had with my father, I tended to try to lighten the situation when it got too deep, and Toby usually played along.

Looked like it'd worked.

"Are you really okay?" Payton asked Aaron softly when he stood up straight.

"I will be. Don't worry about me, doll."

Yeah, the guy was young, he'd be fine. But I knew that sitting around on a Saturday night stewing about shit like that was never a good idea, which was why I said, "Why don't we get out of here for a while?"

"I really shouldn't leave him," Payton told me, clearly assuming I was only talking to her.

"All of us, Payton. I know a place we can go."

"He knows a place," Toby smarted off. "I've heard that before."

Apparently, Chloe was satisfied with Aaron's reassuring statement, because she joined Toby in the living room. She surprised the shit out of us all when she walked right up to him and put her arms around his neck, pulling him close and kissing the shit out of him.

"Get a room," Aaron grumbled, smirking.

Toby wrapped his arms around Chloe, sliding his big hands down to her thighs, then easily lifted her off her feet and turned her toward her bedroom. With her legs wrapped around Toby's hips, Chloe released his lips, slapping his shoulder and laughing.

"But he said… No?" Toby asked, grinning. "Fine. If we don't go in there, we go with him."

Chloe looked down at me. Her green eyes narrowed, her lips quirking slightly as though she was considering the implications of doing just that. And then she smiled. "Fine. I'm game. How bad could it be?"

"You might wanna save that question for later, babe," Toby told her, giving her a quick kiss on the lips before lowering her back to her feet and then smacking her ass.

"Let me change," Chloe said, giggling before darting to her bedroom.

I stood, watching Payton. I could tell she was torn between staying with Aaron and going with us. I wasn't leaving without her, so I said, "Grab a jacket. It'll be cold."

Aaron started down the hall, and I figured he was planning to sneak off to avoid me, so I stopped him with my next statement. "That means you, too, Blondie. Where's your jacket? We've got things to do tonight, and whining like a little fucking girl ain't gonna work."

Aaron spun around and faced me, frowning. The guy really was too fucking pretty. We were probably ten feet apart, and I could see the annoyance in his eyes, but even I could see that he wasn't really pissed at me. He probably wanted to be, but he wasn't. He knew I was joking, even if he didn't know me that well. Because if I hadn't been joking, he wouldn't still be standing there.

"Fine," he groused before turning away again.

"It's settled then. Five minutes," I called after Aaron. "Then we're out."

I glanced at Toby, and he nodded before dropping onto the couch.

When Payton came to my side, I pretended Toby wasn't still there watching us. I pulled her against me and pressed my lips to hers—I couldn't help it. The woman had the most kissable lips. If it were up to me, I'd kiss her all damn night.

I backed my way into her bedroom, fully intending to grab my jacket and something to keep her warm, but I didn't release her lips. I didn't want to.

Stopping just inside her room, I cupped her face with my hands and drew back a little so I could look in her eyes. Her skin was so soft, her eyes reflecting her innocence. Just looking at her unhinged me, made me feel things I'd never thought possible. Rather than a constant state of chaos, the woman filled me with peace. I didn't know how that was possible, but since I'd never experienced it before, I knew it was something about her. Just her.

Remembering our conversation from earlier and the fact that we'd let it drop when Aaron had stormed into Payton's apartment unannounced, I figured now would be the time to make sure she wasn't ready to toss my ass out. Probably good to know before I went any further.

"You okay with what I told you earlier?" I asked, keeping my voice low so Toby couldn't hear.

Payton briefly closed her eyes and sighed. "Conrad's your father."

Her eyes slid open, and she met my gaze, obviously waiting for a reply. I nodded.

"Why is it such a big secret?" she asked, her hazel eyes narrowing on my face.

I really didn't want to get into the details yet. My story wasn't one you'd tell if you were expecting to have a pleasant evening. I was willing to tell her whatever she wanted to know, but I wasn't sure now was the time to go into more detail. Especially not when there were people waiting on us.

"That part's not so easy to explain," I told her, sliding my knuckles along her cheek. Damn, I loved touching her. When Payton started to say something, I put my fingers to her lips and continued, "But I will if you want me to."

I could hear Chloe's voice coming from the other room. She was laughing at something Toby said. Payton glanced over her shoulder and then back at me. "Promise we'll pick up where we left off earlier?"

"I promise." There was plenty more we needed to talk about where Conrad was concerned, especially since Payton worked for him, but now wasn't the right time. "Does that mean we can put kissing back on the table?"

"Maybe." She touched my face with her hands, and I pressed my forehead to hers, relishing the smoothness of her skin against mine, the way her fingers left tingles in their wake.

"Good. 'Cause I plan to do a lot of that tonight."

"That's what I was hoping you'd say."

I pressed a kiss to her nose and reluctantly released her to retrieve my jacket from the chair where I'd left it earlier. If we kept this up, I would forget all other plans in lieu of spending the night alone with her.

Shrugging into my jacket, I turned to face her. She was still watching me.

"What's wrong?"

"Nothing," she replied, looking sad. "It's just… About Conrad, I don't—"

Two steps forward and I stopped her midsentence, placing my fingers on her lips again. "I know you've got questions. And I've got plenty of answers. But maybe we can table them for a bit. Let's get out of here. Have some fun tonight." I moved my fingers and kissed her gently before cupping her face and tilting her head so she looked at me. "I'll tell you anything, Angel. Anything you wanna know. And if you want to close that door and bombard me with question after question, I'll even answer them now. But I can tell you, it won't be a fun conversation. For either of us. So what do you say we go out with them" — I tipped my chin toward the other room — "and we'll pick up where we left off later."

"Promise?"

"Swear," I assured her.

Payton nodded, and I took the opportunity to steal one more kiss, unable to keep my hands off her. I cupped her ass and pulled her against me, showing her just what she did to me. When I pulled back, we were both breathless and her face was flushed.

It took everything in my power to walk out of that room. I would have preferred to shut the door and toss her on the bed.

But that would have to come later.

That, I could definitely promise.

Chapter Two

Sebastian

Twenty minutes later, after Aaron grabbed his jacket from his little girly car and Chloe and Payton argued with him in the darkened apartment complex parking lot about who he would ride with, the three of them finally decided that Aaron would go with us.

Watching him cram his tall, lanky body into the backseat of my Camaro had me holding back a laugh. Not that Toby's car would've provided more leg room. Toby had arrived in his '69 Camaro SS, and when I quietly informed him where I intended to go, his face had lit up like a kid on Christmas morning. Without a word, he had dragged Chloe to his car and helped her in, his eyes continuing to dart back to me. He was excited, there was no doubt about that.

The mood in my car was somber, thanks to Aaron and his pissy attitude. Payton wasn't talking much, either, so I didn't have to tell either of them where we were going. No one had questioned the fact that we were taking two cars, either. Then again, it wasn't like we could have taken one car in the first place. No one had one big enough to hold five people comfortably, so taking two made sense, and I wanted to keep our destination a secret for a little while longer.

When everyone was safely inside their respective vehicle, I made my way out of the parking lot, took a left toward the toll road. Hitting the entrance ramp at eighty, I headed south, back toward my house, but I had no intention of going home. I wanted to show Payton something, and this was the perfect opportunity. The fact that Toby was there was only an added bonus.

I was just about to turn up the radio to fill some of the deafening silence in the car when Payton rotated in her seat and looked back at Aaron. I darted a glance her way, then checked on Aaron in the rearview mirror.

Oh, crap.

I didn't know every one of Payton's expressions just yet, but I did know women. That look meant she wasn't at all ready to drop the discussion from earlier. She was clearly curious, and she was ready to ask questions.

I kind of felt sorry for Aaron.

Kind of.

"So, what happened?" Payton's question was as loaded as they came, which I found comical. Glancing in the rearview mirror again, I saw Aaron roll his eyes, but he wasn't smiling. He clearly wasn't much on talking about the event that had caused his earlier tirade, but I got the feeling Payton was persistent, which was the main reason he looked like he was ready to give in.

"Mark's a bastard."

"Well, that's a given," Payton agreed. "But that doesn't tell me what he did."

A heavy sigh sounded from the backseat. I grinned at Aaron's obvious discomfort, but I kept my eyes on the road, trying to keep my speed to a reasonable level. That was often difficult for me to do, especially when we hit the toll road. With a speed limit of eighty, going over one hundred was relatively easy for me. But, for Payton's sake, I kept it closer to ninety. As it was, we hadn't been in the car long, and she'd kept her hand firmly on the *oh shit* handle until just now.

"We were supposed to go out tonight," Aaron explained sadly. "Or so I thought. We made plans last weekend, when I stayed the night after the party."

My thoughts drifted back to that party and the way Aaron had hauled Payton out of there after practically throwing my jacket that she'd been wearing in my face. I grinned to myself. He had purposely made me believe they were together. Sly bastard. As understanding dawned, I realized he'd been playing me then. Keeping Payton away from me made her all the more desirable — or so he'd probably thought at the time. Little did he know, but I'd already set out with the intention of making her mine. His interference hadn't been necessary, but it proved he did care about her.

"When I called him earlier in the week," Aaron continued, "he kinda blew me off, but I thought it was because he was busy. He told me work was kicking his ass, so I tried to ease off."

"Man, tell me you didn't just go over there unannounced?" I asked, figuring it was my car so, by default, I was part of the conversation.

"I did," Aaron admitted, glaring at me in the rearview mirror.

"Dumbass," I said teasingly.

As I watched in the mirror, Aaron flipped me off from the backseat.

"Was he...?" Payton asked, her hand coming up to cover her mouth when Aaron didn't elaborate.

"Yep. Right there in his bed."

19

"What did he say when you caught him?" Payton asked, twisting in her seat so she could see him better.

Aaron didn't answer right away, and I glanced in the mirror again, waiting. I was just as interested in hearing the answer. If it'd been me and I'd walked in on some chick I was dating to find her in bed with another guy, I would have beaten the shit out of him.

Not that I thought Aaron was the type of guy to speak with his fists. Pretty boys didn't usually do that shit. Not to mention, Aaron looked considerably more reasonable than I was.

"He said he was sorry. A little difficult to believe when he was wrapped around another guy."

Payton laughed, but the sound was strangled. I could tell she was pissed for her friend. Hell, I was pissed for him and I didn't even know the guy.

"Did he at least try to stop you?" she asked.

"Yeah. I told him to get fucked," Aaron said, chuckling, obviously acknowledging the double entendre.

"Seriously, man. That's bullshit." Again, I joined in the conversation just because I could.

I didn't know Aaron all that well, but it was evident that he and Payton were close. I figured if I had any chance with her, it wouldn't hurt to get on her friend's good side.

"So I stormed out. And that's when I came home."

I nearly drove off the road. "Wait. What?" I jerked my head over to look at Payton. "Home?"

When she shrugged, I glanced in the rearview mirror to see Aaron looking back at me, smiling. His grin lit up his entire face. "She didn't tell you? I live with her."

Great.

Payton turned toward me. "We've been roommates since our sophomore year of college."

Double great.

"I've known her since junior high. And no, I'm not her boyfriend now, and I never was in the past, either," Aaron confirmed, laughing.

"I kinda got that part." And it was only because the dude was gay that I didn't pull off the road and drop his ass on the side of the highway.

We were halfway to our destination when my cell phone rang. I knew who it was without looking. Toby had a big fucking mouth, and I knew he wouldn't be able to resist. I figured he'd probably waited three minutes before calling Leif, but that would've been the longest. Toby was the last person you would ever want to share a secret with. He wouldn't last five minutes before sharing the news with anyone who would listen.

I dug for my phone in my jacket pocket and glanced at the screen. Yep. I was right.

Toby had a big fucking mouth.

Knowing Leif would kick my ass if I didn't answer, I hit the talk button and put the phone to my ear. Less than a minute later, I was tossing the phone on the seat.

"Who was that?" Payton asked, turning in her seat to face me.

"Leif."

"What did he want?"

Enjoying Payton's nosiness, I cast a look in her direction and smiled. "He doesn't want to be left out."

"Of?"

"You'll see."

Clearly she had no idea what I was talking about, but surprisingly she didn't ask any more questions. At least not of me. As for Aaron, he got pummeled with questions, most of them having to do with Mark.

Fifteen minutes later, I exited the highway with Toby less than a car length behind me.

"Where are we?" Payton asked when we turned off on a back road.

I nodded toward the south. "Your office is about five miles that way."

"So why are we here?" she asked after glancing out the window into the dark.

"One of my buddies has a track. He lets me use it whenever I want. He hasn't had a race there for a couple of years."

I'd considered buying the place when Stu Strickland had stopped holding races but had talked myself out of it due to the location. Part of me was grateful for my fear of commitment, because I'd recently located an even better location farther north. In fact, I'd shot off a text earlier in the day to a real estate buddy of mine to put in an offer. I wasn't usually one to make big decisions when I was pissed, but after fighting with Conrad, I'd come to one final conclusion: I was done with the bullshit.

And now, if things worked out the way I hoped they would, I'd be gearing up to build something bigger and better than the deserted track we were about to embark upon. Although the place was abandoned, the track was still in great shape.

"Race? As in cars?" Aaron asked from the backseat.

"Yep," I confirmed.

"Thank God," Aaron said on a deep exhale. "I was praying you weren't taking us to some redneck bar."

"Not into that sort of thing?" I countered, trying to imagine Aaron in a redneck bar.

"Not usually, no."

"Then we'll get along just fine. I don't care for them, either. But don't tell Toby that. He's a redneck. Those types of places are like his second home."

"Is that…?" Payton's question trailed off as we pulled into the eroded parking lot a minute later.

"Leif? Yeah." I wasn't surprised to see him there already. He'd been at his mother's house, where he still lived, which wasn't far from the track. My guess was that he'd broken the sound barrier in an attempt to get there before we did. The guy was as competitive as I was.

I drove across the potholed parking lot to where Leif was waiting in his fancy-ass Mustang. Pulling up beside him, I told Payton and Aaron to stay put while I unlocked the gates. After pushing the eight-foot-tall, chain link fence open, I made my way back to the car while Toby and Leif pulled through first. I wasn't far behind.

A few more minutes passed while I pulled in and locked the gates behind us, then ventured to a small building where the control panels were. After flipping on the track lights, I returned to the car to find Payton and Aaron waiting patiently. Then, finally, I was driving down the narrow concrete path to the track.

"You aren't gonna race right now, are you?" Payton asked, her hazel eyes wide as she stared over at me. The blue glow from the dashboard cast her face in shadows, but I could see the curiosity there.

"Not yet," I told her truthfully, smiling to myself.

I fully intended to race — after all, why waste a perfectly good opportunity — but even I wasn't crazy enough to do that with her in the car. For now, I was content just being with her. This place was isolated, quiet, which meant it was the perfect spot to just chill. It was one of the few spots I came to hang out these days. Most of the time I came alone, though, so this was a nice change of pace.

When we reached the overgrown grassy area that surrounded the track, I pulled off. Leif and Toby parked their cars relatively close to mine, everyone piling out. I glanced back at Leif's '06 Mustang in time to see him and his brother getting out. I wanted to laugh, but I knew no one else would have any clue why I was, so I kept my amusement to myself. After all, no one could have planned it better.

Coincidences like this just didn't happen every day.

"Took you long enough," Leif smirked as he strode toward me when I opened Payton's door to help her out. "Was your grandma drivin'?"

"Fuck off," I muttered, grinning. "You better enjoy the feeling while you can. It's the only time you'll beat me."

Leif laughed and his brother slapped him on the back when he joined us. Toby and Chloe weren't far behind, and when everyone gathered around my car, I made the necessary introductions. "Payton, remember Leif? And this is his brother, Garth."

"Man, fuck you. My name ain't Garth," Garrett retorted without heat, his distinct Texas drawl making me smile. "Name's Garrett. Don't listen to this asshole."

Payton laughed as she eased against my side, reaching out to take Garrett's proffered hand. I wrapped my arm around her shoulder and pulled her against me. The sweet scent of her hair instantly soothed the riot that was still clamoring in my brain.

I wanted her more than I wanted air, and it was killing me to hold back. I wasn't used to dating a girl prior to sleeping with her. In fact, I didn't usually date, period. But with Payton, taking her to bed wasn't the first thing that came to mind when I thought about her. Although, it was a close second.

"Nice to meet you," Payton said shyly, shaking Garrett's hand. "These are my roommates, Chloe and Aaron."

I watched with voyeuristic fascination as Garrett shook Chloe's hand and then Aaron's, his eyes slowly trailing from Chloe to Aaron. Yep, just like I suspected, instant chemistry.

Garrett Connelly, who I liked to call Garth, was the kind of guy who women flocked to like flies to honey. He was one of those people who caused crowds to part when he walked through. Big guy. Six four. He would've been lanky if it weren't for the muscle that lined his lean frame. He looked a lot like Leif, just a few inches taller and wider.

Just like all four of the Connelly brothers, Leif and Garrett sported the same dark hair and dark brown eyes. Neither of them regularly shaved, so they were always sporting a scruffy jaw. Garth was a couple of years older than Leif, who was the youngest Connelly and the same age as me. At twenty-seven, Garrett was the only one of Leif's brothers who hadn't ventured into the automotive industry. Garrett was a drummer. One of the best I'd ever heard. I called him Garth because back when he was in high school, he had aspired to be a country music singer. A phase, he called it.

"Didn't know you were in town," I said to Garrett as I watched him watch Aaron.

Oh, did I mention Garrett was gay? Well, bisexual was probably a better term for it, but it seemed Garrett preferred the same sex, for the most part, although he'd been known to bag some of the groupies, too.

Like I said, coincidence.

"For a few days," Garrett answered, finally looking back at me. "Then we're back on the road."

Toby walked over and slapped Garrett on the back. "What's up, Garth?"

Garrett elbowed Toby in the gut, making him grunt as he bent over. "Nice to see you, too, dude."

"So, what is this place?" Chloe asked, walking over to stand by Payton, her eyes roaming the darkness that surrounded the track.

"Racetrack," Aaron informed her.

"I got that part, Einstein. Why are we here?"

"To race," Toby said quickly, grinning at her as though he hadn't just stated the obvious, as well.

"No shit?" Aaron asked, glancing around at everyone, his bright blue eyes landing on Garrett. And staying there.

"I'm here to race," I informed them. "Y'all are here to lose. But not yet. Come on."

I took Payton's hand and led everyone down to the track, Toby mumbling something that sounded a lot like, "There's a first time for everything."

I grinned.

For now, I'd show them around. And a little later, I'd show them how it was done.

Chapter Three

Payton

If I said that I would've ever thought I'd be standing in the middle of a deserted racetrack at night with Sebastian close by, I'd be lying. Heck, standing on a deserted racetrack at all was so far out of my element I was having a hard time keeping up.

But Sebastian *was* there with me, his arm wrapped tightly around my shoulders as we walked from the grassy knoll down to the track. The way he kept me close, insisting on touching me at all times, was incredibly comforting. And strangely erotic. If it hadn't been for everyone else being there, it would've been romantic.

When we'd left the apartment a short time ago, I wasn't sure what I had expected. A sports bar, maybe. Pizza place, possibly. I certainly hadn't anticipated this.

It was something out of a movie, and if Sebastian hadn't unlocked the gates in front of me, I would've thought we were trespassing. Except he looked as though he was used to being there. And that settled some of my nerves.

But Sebastian was right. It might not be a place that saw many people these days, but it seemed in relatively good shape. The grass surrounding and through the middle of the track hadn't been cut in a while, but that was about the only clue that no one spent time there.

As we walked down the steep embankment to the asphalt, I was trying to take it all in. Sebastian's nearness, our friends talking and joking, the overhead lights brightening the area as though it were daytime. I felt almost like I was intoxicated, but I hadn't had a drop of alcohol, so I knew that wasn't the case. Part of me kept waiting to wake up to find that this was some sort of crazy dream. I mean, I was still reeling from Sebastian showing up at my apartment, and then the odd conversation we'd been having when Aaron interrupted.

If it hadn't been for the others moving about, laughing — mainly at Toby and his antics — I would've considered pinching myself to see if I woke up. Then again, if this was a dream, I wasn't sure I wanted to.

Even with everyone causing a pleasant distraction, I was still having a hard time keeping myself from staring at Sebastian. He might not know it, but he was the center of the attraction — and not just for me. It seemed that everyone enjoyed being around him. Leif and Toby were constantly getting his attention, pulling him into the conversation. I noticed they were especially attentive when Sebastian grew quiet. It was as though they didn't want him to get lost in his own head, even for a little while.

He wasn't an easy person to ignore. Not that I'd tried.

He just seemed larger than life, so enigmatic and intense. And I was drawn to him. When he was anywhere in the vicinity, it was as though I forgot about everything and everyone else. Aaron was just lucky that I loved him as much as I did, because deserting Sebastian to check on him earlier hadn't been an easy thing for me to do. I wanted to spend every minute with Sebastian.

Sebastian's unexpected arrival at my apartment had started a chain of unexpected events, which had led to me standing on a racetrack with the uber sexy guy who'd plagued my every thought since the day I'd met him. It wasn't easy to pretend not to be affected by him, either. When he put his arm around my shoulders, pulling me close, I could smell the delicious scent of his cologne mixed with the wonderful smell of leather. He was overwhelming my senses. The way he was constantly touching me made my skin tingle. I could feel the heat of his body everywhere. And the simple fact that he kept me close to him made me feel as though I'd known him all my life when, really, we hardly knew one another.

He made my body burn, and I was already contemplating whether or not I was going to ask him to stay the night tonight. I didn't know if he would consider it too early in our relationship for what I had in mind, but I wasn't sure how much longer I could wait, either. That was one of the first signs that I was in over my head with him, because I certainly wasn't the type of girl who was generally ruled by my hormones, but there was something about Sebastian. My head was filled with crazy ideas whenever I thought about him. Even more so when I was near him.

For whatever reason, whether because he was a gentleman or possibly something else, Sebastian seemed to be refraining from going too far with me, which had me questioning my own desires.

And to see this side of him… It was more than I could handle.

Although we'd been having a serious conversation and he'd dropped the father bomb on me earlier, he had been a good sport when Aaron had come barreling into the apartment ready to tear it to shreds because he'd caught his boyfriend cheating.

As soon as Aaron had mentioned Mark's name, it had been a no-brainer that I had to spend the evening with Aaron. After all, he was my best friend and he needed me. I just hadn't expected Sebastian to want to hang out, as well. But somehow he'd managed to lighten the mood and then turn it around completely.

Knowing Aaron, he would've preferred to sit at home and wallow in his hurt, but Sebastian hadn't given him much of a choice. Actually, Sebastian hadn't given him a choice at all.

Which was why we were standing on a racetrack, listening to Leif and Toby argue over the official terminology for everything. They were bantering back and forth like children, Toby interrupting to correct Leif whenever he could. Everyone was laughing. Everyone except Sebastian, who was constantly looking around, aware of everything around him, not just his friends.

Although the track intrigued me, I was more interested in watching Sebastian. The way he moved, the way he spoke. He was a dichotomy. I knew there was something dark and dangerous lurking inside him, because I'd seen a glimpse of it, but here, tonight, with his friends and mine, it wasn't as noticeable.

When Sebastian had arrived at my apartment earlier, he'd been upset. Actually, angry was a better way to describe his demeanor when he'd arrived unexpectedly. The little make-out session we'd had in my bedroom had helped ease some of the tension, but this certainly wasn't the direction I'd seen the night going. Sebastian had done a complete turnaround just because Aaron had needed someone to cheer him up. And for that reason, among other things, I had a sneaking suspicion that I was quickly falling for him.

Okay, that wasn't entirely true. I don't think there was any suspicion. I was falling for Sebastian Trovato. Fast and hard. And surprisingly, that didn't bother me in the least. Being with Sebastian felt right.

While everyone laughed and joked, Sebastian remained close to my side, one arm wrapped around my shoulders, the other crossing over in front of me, the fingers of his right hand linked with my left. With my head resting against his chest, his mouth frequently brushed my hair as he spoke. It was intimate, and so natural. I felt safe in his arms.

I paid attention to the way he interacted with Toby and Leif. It was apparent that they had a close friendship. They teased in a way that only good friends could do, and from what I'd seen so far, they were always having a good time when they were together, even though Sebastian's intensity hadn't lessened any.

"Are you cold?" Sebastian asked, turning his attention to me while Toby and Leif continued to rib one another good-naturedly.

"No." I wasn't cold. In fact, I was rather warm, and it had nothing to do with the jacket Sebastian had insisted that I bring, either. "Thanks for doing this, by the way."

"Happy to. I'm just glad you're here with me," Sebastian said, his voice soft and low.

"Me, too." He would never know how happy I was about that. If I had my way, I'd never be apart from him. And I knew that we hadn't known each other long enough for me to feel that way, but time didn't even seem to be relevant when we were together. I felt like I'd known him for a lot longer than just a little more than a week.

"So, Garrett, you said you were only in town for a couple of days?" Chloe's question had me engaging in the conversation, curious as to what had brought it on. "What is it that you do?"

Garrett glanced over at Leif, then to Sebastian, but Toby was the one who answered. "He's in a band."

"Which one?" Chloe asked, her eyes widening.

As though he felt the need to stake his claim, Toby made his way to Chloe's side, gently pulling her against him.

"Heat Seekers," Garrett replied.

"Are you freaking serious?" Chloe exclaimed. "Oh, my God!"

The girl's excitement meter had just redlined. I had no idea who the Heat Seekers were, but apparently she did. That or she was just strangely excited by the name.

"I saw y'all play at Stubb's last year. Wow. Small world. Great show, by the way."

"Thanks." Garrett looked a little bashful, which surprised me. Then again, his appearance surprised me, too. He looked so … normal. Aside from the tattoos coloring his forearms — the only part of his body I could see besides his neck and head — he didn't look like a rock star. He was very clean-cut with his short dark hair and lack of piercings. Even the scruffy jaw looked more preppy than rugged.

I noticed Aaron was watching Garrett as though the guy had just announced he was on the cover of *People* magazine and had just been named sexiest man alive.

"So are we gonna get our race on or what?" Leif interrupted.

"Dude, quit bein' a baby," Toby interjected. "Just 'cause my girl's droolin' over your brother doesn't mean you gotta speak up. We like you better when you're quiet."

Leif elbowed Toby this time, making him grunt. "Y'all are gonna have to stop doin' that shit."

"I was thinking that Toby should be the one worried," Aaron said. "Chloe's got that wild look in her eyes."

Chloe merely smiled at Aaron. I could tell she was a little star struck by Garrett, but that look was nothing compared to the look she gave Toby every chance she could.

"Seriously," Leif stated. "We gonna do this?"

"In a minute," Sebastian answered, smiling down at me as though he were waiting for me to tell him that it was okay.

"I wanna watch you race," I whispered, the adrenaline from everyone's enthusiasm coursing through me. I had to admit, the idea of watching Sebastian race was sexy as hell.

"You heard the lady," Toby called out. "She wants to watch."

Chapter Four

Payton

A few minutes later, Sebastian released me from the circle of his arms, but he kept his fingers linked with mine as we made our way up into the stands, the others following close behind. When we reached the top of the stairs, he let me take the lead, still holding my hands behind me and directing me with ease.

When we reached the section of the stands in front of the starting line, Sebastian stopped.

"Kiss for good luck," he demanded, turning me around to face him as he cupped my face in his big, warm hands.

I definitely had no intention of arguing. Going up on my toes, I met his lips with mine, loving the way the metal from his lip ring slid across my lower lip. The hunger returned, and I wrapped my arms around his neck, not caring where we were or who was watching. I wanted this man with a passion I didn't understand. When he slipped his tongue in my mouth, I raked mine over his, the barbell through his tongue making me even crazier with lust. He was so damn sexy.

"Get a room!" Aaron shouted from somewhere behind me.

Sebastian smiled against my mouth and pulled back, leaving me feeling a little dazed. My heart was racing, and it wasn't just because of Sebastian's kisses. Although that was a huge part of it.

Sebastian steered me to a bench and ordered me to sit, so I did. "Don't move."

"Yes, sir," I retorted, saluting him.

He then leaned down and pressed his lips to mine one more time. He didn't linger, and part of me was disappointed. I could've kissed him all night, but I knew it was going to eventually lead to something more. I was ready. Too ready, so I admired Sebastian's self-control. He had managed to pull us back from the brink when I was ready to jump in with both feet.

Did that make me a bad person? I'd only known him for a week, yet I felt like I'd known him my entire life, and getting naked with the sexiest man on the planet had suddenly become one of my only goals in life. That should've freaked me out, but as I watched Sebastian walk away, I couldn't bring myself to care. The guy was absolutely gorgeous.

Chloe joined me on the bench, scooting close to my side, linking her arm with mine and snuggling against me. Aaron and Garrett were deep in conversation, leaning against the rails in front of us.

"Is this hot or what?" Chloe asked, her excitement palpable.

"Pretty hot." Anything that had to do with Sebastian was hot, though. At least in my opinion.

"I'm gonna ask Toby to stay the night," Chloe mentioned, her voice low enough that only I could hear.

I jerked my head to the side to look at her. "You mean he hasn't already?"

Chloe shook her head. "Not yet."

Thinking about what that meant, I narrowed my eyes at her. "Are you ... sure?"

I had known from the night we'd seen Sebastian at the sports bar that Chloe was captivated by Toby. And then when I'd found him sitting in my kitchen just that morning, I'd known she was serious about him. They were cute together, I'd give them that. I hadn't been around them much, but they did seem to enjoy one another's company. I just didn't want to see my friend jump in too fast. Chloe was impulsive, but usually not when it came to men. Then again, I was contemplating doing the same thing, and we were very much alike in that regard. In my defense, I'd known Sebastian a little longer. Granted, I had only seen him once during the first week of knowing him, but it was still technically longer.

"I really like him," Chloe answered. "I mean *really* like him, Payton."

I turned back to watch the guys getting into their cars, resting my head against Chloe's. "Just be careful. And I'm not just talking about safe sex," I clarified.

"I'll do my best."

Chloe was a lot like me in the sense that she didn't date often. Admiring guys from afar was what we usually did, both of us too busy to deal with relationships. But during the time I'd known Chloe, she had been in two serious relationships, both of them ending badly. I hated to see my friend hurt, but more selfishly, if things didn't work out for her and Toby … that could potentially have negative implications on my relationship with Sebastian.

The rev of Sebastian's engine as he slowly drove down to the track wrenched me from my thoughts. Sebastian's glossy black Camaro was followed by Leif's fire-engine-red Mustang and Toby's matte black, older-model Camaro pulled up the rear as they made their way back onto the pavement. All three cars would have blended with the night if it weren't for the sports lights that lit up the area like it was daytime.

From where I sat in the bleachers, I was looking down at the track. Admittedly, I wasn't much of a racing fan. I didn't follow NASCAR, nor did I watch Formula One, although Austin had recently built a track for the latter. If there was a regulation size, I didn't know, but this track didn't look like anything I'd seen on television other than it was oval-shaped with four banked corners. Just a few minutes ago, we had been down there, so I knew firsthand just how steep those corners were. My gut twisted as my anticipation mixed with a tiny amount of nervousness.

I held my breath as the three cars started down the track. They weren't going fast, and from what I knew of racing, which was very, very little, I figured they were warming up their tires first. That was something my father always warned me about, considering it had been his bright idea to put Pirellis on my Mustang. For what purpose, I would never know. But I knew firsthand that when they were cold, they were slick on the pavement.

And that's exactly what the three cars did for a few laps, weaving back and forth across the track, keeping their speed to a minimum. I watched, admiring the American muscle. All three cars were impressive. I happened to be partial to Sebastian's, but that was because it was Sebastian's. I still remembered the first time I'd seen it. I'd been so nervous, the name of the car hadn't come to me.

When they pulled to a stop at the starting line, I held my breath.

Chloe squeezed my arm, her legs bouncing, her feet tapping the concrete beneath us.

"My money's on Sebastian," Garrett said, his deep voice carrying on the chilly night air.

"Why's that?" Aaron asked.

"The guy's never lost."

Really?

That made my heart swell with pride. Why, I had no idea.

As I watched, eagerly waiting for them to start, I realized I was still smiling. By the time the night was out, I was sure my cheeks were going to hurt.

And then they were off. I had no idea how they determined when to go, but all three engines revved, and then they peeled off the starting line, the front ends surging forward, all that horsepower flooding the night with a sexy rumble.

Chloe squealed, squeezing my arm tightly. My body buzzed and hummed, the intensity of the moment sending a flurry of butterflies through my tummy.

Once they got going, I only had eyes for Sebastian's Camaro. He steadily gained speed until he was flying around the track, going up the banked corners and then back down the straightaways, the other two cars close behind him. The faster he went, the tighter my hands clenched, until the circulation in my fingers was cut off. I was gritting my teeth, and I could feel the adrenaline coursing through me although I wasn't the one in the car.

"How fast are they going?" Chloe shouted to Garrett and Aaron.

"I'd say ... about one thirty. Maybe one forty," Garrett replied.

"Holy shit."

Yep, holy shit was right.

I was so enthralled by the action I had no idea how much time had passed before Sebastian slowed after crossing the finish line one last time. He'd won, just as Garrett had said.

"That was fucking awesome!" Chloe screeched, jumping to her feet and making her way down to where Aaron and Garrett were standing. I didn't get up, mostly because I wasn't sure I could. I was still reeling from watching Sebastian.

Toby, Leif, and Sebastian razzed each other as they made their way back to the stands, all three of them laughing. Toby took Sebastian in a headlock and rubbed his knuckles over Sebastian's head. Yeah, it didn't seem to matter to the three of them who had won. It was the thrill of the race that apparently got them off.

To each his own.

I couldn't take my eyes off Sebastian. Right there, at that moment, he looked like my wildest fantasy come to life. His hair was mussed, his smile wide. He must have ditched his jacket in the car, because I could see his tattoos peeking out beneath the sleeves of his T-shirt, his biceps pulling the fabric tight. He was breathing heavy, as though he'd just run a mile. I figured that had to do with the adrenaline.

When he met my gaze as he came toward me, I saw the exhilaration there. It was potent. So much so that my body warmed instantly; the chill in the crisp November evening was overshadowed by that heat.

"So?" Sebastian asked when he made his way back to me, stopping a row down and standing in front of me.

"So *what?*" I asked, my voice shaking from my excitement, but I was trying to play it cool.

"What'd you think?"

"Eh," I teased, pretending indifference.

Sebastian leaned back against the rail that ran the length of the bleachers, his foot propped on the lower rung, his elbows resting on the top.

Lord, have mercy, the man made my heart race.

"Oh yeah?" he asked, chuckling. "That good, huh?"

"It was kinda … hot," I admitted, laughing, trying to keep from blushing.

"Wanna try it?" he asked.

"Nope," I said as confidently as I could. I didn't mind watching, actually enjoyed it, but I definitely wasn't a race car type of girl.

"Ready to get out of here?"

I nodded and got to my feet. Sebastian waited for me to go down the stairs first and then followed close, everyone else somewhere behind us. I hoped he didn't see that my hands were shaking. Watching him drive had been incredibly stimulating but nerve-racking all the same.

When we reached his car, he came to the passenger side, but before opening the door, he turned me to face him and backed me against it. Again, without thinking about where we were or who was with us, I wrapped my arms around his waist, sliding my hands beneath his T-shirt so I could feel his heated skin against my palms.

"What did you really think?" he asked softly, peering down at me.

"It was incredible," I admitted breathlessly, pushing up on my toes and pressing my lips to his. I flicked his lip ring gently. "I've never seen anything sexier. Well, besides you."

Sebastian watched me for long seconds, not saying anything. His hands were planted on the roof of the car, one on each side of my head, his rock-solid body pressed into me. I could see his jaw flexing, as though he wanted to say something but thought better of it.

"I hope we're gonna get food after this," Toby said. Who he was talking to, I had no idea. Nor did I care.

"About earlier," Sebastian said on a sigh, those mysterious storm clouds gathering in his golden eyes once again. "About Conrad…"

His statement took me by surprise after all the laughter and joking that had been going on for the last hour. I put my finger against his lips, my eyes locked with his. "We need to talk more. I know that. But you needed this." I don't know how I knew that, but I did. I knew that whatever he had going on in his head, he needed this. He used racing as a release; he'd pretty much told me so.

"I need *you*, Angel," he said, his warm breath fluttering over my lips. "That's all I really need."

My heart beat faster, so fast that I nearly lost my breath. The meaning behind those few words was so much deeper than what I'd expected.

Could it be possible that this was meant to be? That Sebastian and I had been destined to meet? I thought back to the dream I'd had about him before I ever met him, and it was then that I realized that yes, whatever this was, it had been in the cards all along.

"I need you, too," I whispered.

Sebastian rested his forehead against mine briefly.

"Come on, y'all. Let's go eat," Leif called out.

"You hungry?" Sebastian asked, his voice low.

Unable to resist, I answered with something he'd said to me before. "Yeah. But not for food."

"Angel, you're gonna be the death of me." Sebastian chuckled and then pressed his lips to mine quickly before pulling back and opening my door. "Come on, let's go eat."

I nodded my head. I wanted to tell him that I'd much rather take him back to my apartment and feast on him for a little while. But part of me worried that it was too soon. As much as I wanted to go somewhere private and spend the night in his arms, I knew that was something we would have to work up to.

I just secretly hoped it would be sooner rather than later.

Chapter Five

Payton

Dinner consisted of eggs, bacon, and pancakes. Well, for everyone except Toby. He opted for hash browns instead of pancakes, which I found highly entertaining, especially when Sebastian told the story about Toby's first breakfast with Chloe. The decision to go to IHOP had been unanimous, mainly because it was the first restaurant that we'd come to after leaving the track. That was where all seven of us spent the next two hours, crammed into an oversized, semi-circle booth, eating, laughing, and having a good time.

I wasn't sure I'd ever been as happy as I was right then.

Watching the interaction between everyone at the table was amusing. Chloe and Toby were giving one another bedroom eyes, and I was kind of surprised they hadn't opted to forego dinner in lieu of sneaking back to our apartment. Garrett and Aaron were … well, I wasn't sure what they were doing, but if I had to guess, Aaron wasn't thinking about Mark anymore at all.

The two men seemed to have a lot in common: they were both obsessed with Sons of Anarchy, both avoided redneck bars (as Aaron referred to them) if at all possible, and they detested wine. Oh, and they were clearly attracted to one another. Which, by the way, had come as a little bit of a surprise to me.

I didn't claim to have any super sense, or *gaydar*, as some people referred to it, but I had not received any sort of vibe from Garrett that suggested he was gay. It wasn't until we were back in the car on the way to the restaurant that Sebastian had told me. Granted, Sebastian's exact word was bisexual, which had left me both curious and a little concerned for Aaron.

I was happy for Aaron, but also worried. He was my best friend; not to mention, he was incredibly vulnerable right now. Hell, he'd just found his boyfriend in bed with another man. But as much as I wanted to see him happy, I didn't want him to do something he would regret later. I tried to remind myself that he was a grown man; he could make his own decisions.

I just had to keep telling myself that.

After Chloe and I finished our coffee, the check was split three ways, Sebastian picking up the tab for Aaron and me. I thanked him, making sure he knew he didn't have to do that. He insisted, and the look in his eyes said I shouldn't argue with him. So I didn't.

"We're gonna get out of here," Chloe said as she leaned over to me, resting her chin on my shoulder.

"Okay." I wasn't sure what I was supposed to say to that. I knew where they were going; it was evident. Either our apartment or wherever Toby lived.

"See you at home later?" she asked.

Looked like our apartment won the coin toss there.

"Yep."

After saying their good-byes, Chloe and Toby left hand in hand.

Sebastian must've realized I was worried about her because he leaned over and pressed his lips against my ear. "He's a good guy. I swear to that."

"I just don't want to see her get hurt," I told him softly.

"Not to say she'll hurt him," Sebastian said, his breath warm against my ear, "but there's a better chance of him getting hurt first."

I didn't want to see that, either, but I didn't tell Sebastian as much because Leif interrupted our private conversation.

"We're gonna head out and get a beer. Wanna join us?"

Sebastian glanced at me and I shook my head. I was tired. It had been a long day, and I wasn't up for being out all night. It was already midnight, and crawling into bed was starting to sound better and better.

Preferably with Sebastian, but I didn't tell him that.

"No, thanks," Sebastian answered for us. "I'm gonna take her home and then head home myself."

"You coming with us?" I asked Aaron.

"I'm gonna go with them," Aaron informed me, nodding his head toward Garrett.

As much as I wanted to tell him to be careful, too, I bit my tongue and kept my comment to myself. I needed to take my own advice, not dish it out to everyone else.

"We'll bring him home in a coupla hours," Leif added as the three of them stood and offered more good-byes before they headed out the door.

And then we were the only two left at the table.

"You ready to go?" Sebastian asked, his arm sliding around my shoulders.

"As ready as I'll ever be."

Truth was, I was ready to leave the restaurant, but I wasn't ready to leave Sebastian.

Now I just had to figure out how to tell him that.

Half an hour later, Sebastian was pulling into my apartment complex. I was a little sad to see it hadn't taken long to get home. Even though conversation had been minimal for most of the drive, Sebastian had insisted on holding my hand. Oddly, his mere touch had been all that I needed. Words hadn't been necessary, and the silence that ensued was comforting. But now I didn't want to let him go.

He pulled into an empty spot close to my building and shut off the engine. Neither of us moved for what felt like an eternity, and then Sebastian turned to me. I watched him nervously, wishing I could tell him what was on my mind. When his eyes darted down to my lips, I knew what was coming next.

Rather than wait for him to kiss me, I leaned over, sliding my hand behind his neck and pulling him to me. His arms instantly wrapped around me, our lips sliding together. The kiss started out sweet and gentle, yet there was a hum of hunger vibrating just beneath the surface. I didn't have to take the lead that time, because Sebastian thrust his tongue into my mouth and I moaned, giving in to him.

The air in the car warmed several degrees, my body likely the main contributor. When Sebastian's hands slid beneath my T-shirt, his warmth caressing my back, I knew what I had to do. I didn't want to leave him, didn't want to spend the night without him.

But then he was pulling back, his hands disappearing from my body and returning to the steering wheel as he peered out through the slightly fogged windshield.

"Thank you for tonight," he said quietly.

I knew I should've been the one thanking him, but I couldn't get my voice to work. I wanted to invite him upstairs, to take him to my bedroom and pick up where we'd just left off, but I didn't tell him that.

The next thing I knew, Sebastian was exiting the car and walking around to open my door. Feeling slightly dejected, I accepted his hand and allowed him to help me from the car. I was surprised to see that he was going to walk me to my door. Surprised, but not disappointed.

Once we were up the stairs, Sebastian waited while I slid the key in the lock, but he stopped me before I opened the front door. Without hesitation, he spun me around and pressed me against the door, his lips finding mine while his big, callused hands cupped my face. The hunger returned with a vengeance, our lips crashing together, tongues colliding. I melted into him, wrapping my arms around his waist, sliding my hands beneath his T-shirt, where I found the hard muscles underneath. Digging my nails into his skin, I pulled him closer, desperate for more of him. He smelled so good — the rich scent of his cologne mixed with the sultry scent of his leather jacket. It was a heady mixture.

At that moment, I didn't think I would ever get enough, and the thought of him leaving, even for a little while, wasn't making me feel better.

When he pulled back, my lungs were starved for oxygen and my heart was pounding like a drum, loud enough that I was sure he heard it, too.

"I want to invite you in," I whispered nervously.

Sebastian's thumb grazed my cheek as he watched me, his eyes locked with mine. "I *want* you to invite me in."

Did that mean I was supposed to ask? Or was it assumed now that I'd mentioned it? It almost sounded like there was a *but* in there somewhere, so I waited for Sebastian to say something.

It never came, and I swallowed hard, trying to spit the words out. But then words weren't necessary because someone else took care of that for us. From inside my apartment, I heard Chloe moan, followed by, "Damn, baby. Oh, Chloe."

Needless to say, my face turned scarlet.

Sebastian exhaled on a gruff laugh.

And when Chloe screamed Toby's name, I couldn't help but laugh, as well.

Sebastian reached behind me and relocked the door before pulling the keys from the lock and taking my hand. "Come on."

Following him down the stairs once again, I continued to laugh. It was that or cry, but not because I was sad. My best friend was inside my apartment getting it on with Sebastian's friend, and here I was trying to figure out how to convince Sebastian to stay the night with me.

"Where're we going?" I asked when he joined me inside the car.

"My place."

My breath caught in my throat, and I couldn't look away from him.

"Payton, if you don't want to go, say so now."

I could barely make out his face in the darkness, but I studied him anyway. "I want to go," I said, my throat tight with anticipation.

"Are you sure?"

I didn't even hesitate before I replied. "I've never been more sure about anything in my life."

I could see the heat flare in Sebastian's golden eyes, and I knew that we were about to take this to an entirely different level.

And I hadn't been lying when I'd told him that I wanted it.

In fact, I wanted it more than anything.

Chapter Six

Sebastian

By the time I pulled into my garage forty minutes later, I had damn near broken every speed limit, my palms were sweating, and I'd probably lost two pounds just from how hard my heart was thumping in my chest. Honestly, I was surprised my entire body wasn't sweating since it felt as though I'd done a major cardio workout during the drive back to my house. I didn't think it was possible for something to make my adrenaline pump as fast as it did when I was racing, but this pretty much blew that shit out of the water.

I had never once, not even my very first time, been nervous about taking a woman to bed. But Payton wasn't just any woman.

She was everything.

And here I was, taking her back to my place knowing that I should have just left her at her apartment. It would've been the gentlemanly thing to do. She would've probably locked herself in her bedroom and turned on her stereo, effectively drowning out Chloe and Toby, but I couldn't leave her there.

Okay, so *couldn't* was probably a little strong of a word. I didn't want to. That was more accurate. Anything to keep Payton with me.

So, during the painfully long drive back to my house, I had fought every single thought that filled my head, every one of them revolving around all the things I wanted to do to her when I got her naked.

If I got her naked.

I was beginning to second-guess my decision to bring Payton back to my house, recalling the argument I'd had with my father earlier. It wouldn't bode well for me if Conrad decided to interfere with my relationship with Payton. And I damn sure didn't want him trying to use what might happen between us against me.

"Nice," Payton said when the garage door closed behind us, pulling me from my negative train of thought. I mean, seriously … I had Payton there with me. Thoughts of my father — negative or otherwise — weren't conducive to my current frame of mind.

"What? The house? Or the cars?" I asked, trying to focus on the present.

"Both. Do you live out here?"

I glanced through the windshield, trying to see the garage as she did for the first time. There were couches and chairs sitting in one corner, a refrigerator and sink on the far wall. The rest of the space was filled with either my vehicles or my tools. Yeah, I guess it kind of did look like I lived out there. "I spend a lot of time out here," I told her.

"I can tell," she said, smiling. "What is that?"

I looked over to see her staring out the passenger window at the white car parked next to us.

"Ferrari 458 Spider."

"Wow. Do you drive it?" Payton cast me a sideways glance while she waited for me to answer.

"On occasion." I chuckled, pushing open my door and climbing out, taking a deep breath as I walked around to her side. Opening her door, I inhaled sharply again.

This was actually happening. Payton was at my house. My house.

Well, technically, the place I called home wasn't mine. It belonged to my father, but I'd lived there since the day I'd turned eighteen. I would've left altogether, except Conrad had insisted that I stay in the guesthouse, probably his way of keeping me under his thumb a little while longer. His excuse had been that I needed to be close if I expected to be able to work from the house. It was that or he was going to insist that I go to the shop, which was something I refused to do.

I briefly thought about the house that I was in the process of buying and wished like hell that I was taking Payton there, rather than here. Unfortunately, this place would have to do for now.

We were alone and there wasn't a chance for anyone to interrupt us. Well, unless my asshole of a father decided to invade the guesthouse. Since he hadn't done so up to this point, I held out hope that he would stay away tonight.

Pretty soon I wouldn't have to worry about him invading my space. That was another reason I was moving. Well, that and clearly it was time that I took control of my own life. As much as I liked the convenience of living and working on the Trovato estate, it was time for me to make a stand. For the last few months, my relationship with my father had started deteriorating beyond repair, and it was only getting worse with every day that passed.

Brushing off the thoughts of Conrad, I took Payton's hand and led her through the crowded garage. She was gazing around, checking everything out. I opened the door to the house and stepped back so she could go in before me.

Once inside, I felt a little more at ease. After all, there were no expectations. I just wanted Payton there with me. Even if it meant we spent the rest of the night watching movies on the couch.

When I walked inside, the noise in my head grew a little louder. It was the house. The fact that I hated being there was making me crazy. Again, another good reason that I was finally going to do something about it. Unfortunately, these things took time. I'd been eyeing a particular house for a while, which was the only reason the paperwork was now underway. That decision was the only logical one I'd made all day, with the exception of showing up unannounced at Payton's.

And bringing her back there with me.

She had single-handedly calmed the riot in my head that afternoon when I had shown up at her apartment. It had been a little iffy there for a while, my anger had been a firestorm burning out of control, but just as I'd suspected, the moment I'd looked at her, I had calmed down. Didn't mean I had completely forgotten about the argument I'd had with Conrad, but it went a long way toward keeping me from stewing about it, letting it fester into something that would ultimately tear me apart from the inside out.

I slid off my leather jacket and tossed it on the back of a chair and then helped Payton remove hers, leaving it beside mine.

She was looking up at the twenty-foot-high ceilings that spanned most of the downstairs and then over at the wall of windows that made up the outside of the house when she finally said, "This is … beautiful, Sebastian."

I figured she was referring to the house based on the way she was looking around, but I pretended to misunderstand. "Yes, you are." I eased up behind her, sliding my hands into the front pockets of her jeans and pulling her against me.

The instant we touched, my body reacted to her nearness, the chaos dwindling, immediately replaced with something equally distracting: a desperate, aching need for this woman. It was impossible to control my reaction to her. Just her simple touch made me hard, made me eager to have her in every possible way imaginable. And I knew I wouldn't be able to hide it from her for long, if at all. I could hardly control myself around this woman. Each time I saw her, my craving for her only intensified until it was a conflagration threatening to get out of control.

Not that I wanted her to know that.

Yet.

"Want a tour?" I asked, pressing my lips to the soft skin of her neck.

"Yeah," she said, sounding a little breathless.

Reluctantly, I released her so I could show her around. It wasn't that I wanted to give her a grand tour of the house I would be moving out of in the near future, but it was that or toss her over my shoulder and carry her to my bedroom. I wasn't a patient man, but with Payton, I knew I had to make a concession. The last thing I wanted to do was scare her off.

So, we made our way to the kitchen. I didn't use the area often, mainly because I wasn't much of a cook, and living alone, it just wasn't a place I spent a lot of time. The stainless steel appliances were state-of-the-art and picked out by my stepmother. They looked good with the modern white cabinets and black granite countertops, also designed by Lauren. The decorations that sat on the tops of the counters weren't my idea, either, but since the housekeeper dusted and cleaned once a week, I didn't bother to toss them into a cabinet. Like I said, this was the room I probably spent the least amount of time in.

"What's in your refrigerator?" Payton asked, grinning at me before releasing my hand.

"Are you hungry?" I asked, confused by her question.

"Nope. But what's in the refrigerator tells a lot about a person."

"That right?" I'd never heard that before.

And I wasn't sure the few things in my refrigerator were going to say a lot about me. Especially since I didn't do my own grocery shopping, either.

"Orange juice, yogurt, milk, cheese … water." Payton glanced back at me, her waist-length dark hair sliding over her shoulder and falling down her back. Her smile was radiant, and I knew right then that I wanted to see her in my kitchen more often. Not so that she could cook for me or any sexist bullshit like that, just because she made the space that much more welcoming.

"What does that say about me?" I asked, hopping up onto the counter and watching her.

"It says you're boring, Sebastian."

I chuckled, continuing to watch her rummage through the contents. "Boring, huh?"

"No beer?"

"I don't drink that much. Usually only when I go out." I hadn't bothered to mention to Payton that I had a highly addictive personality, which was the reason I avoided certain things. I didn't drink much, rarely at home; I didn't smoke, although I'd stupidly done so to be cool when I was younger. I'd never tried drugs, either. My drug of choice was adrenaline, which was why I raced. I released the pent-up anger by beating the shit out of the heavy bag in my weight room, knowing that if I didn't, the undercurrent would eventually invade my life and turn me into someone I didn't want to look at in the mirror each day.

"Interesting."

I wanted to know just what was going through her head, but I didn't get to ask because she was on a roll.

"Do you eat cereal?" Payton closed the refrigerator door and opened the freezer.

"Sometimes. Would that make me less boring?"

"Maybe. At least you've got ice cream."

"I do?" I really had no idea.

"Vanilla," she said, grinning widely. "Imagine that."

"I'll have to remember to add chocolate to the grocery list," I told her, remembering the first time I'd taken her out for ice cream.

"You do that. Get chocolate syrup while you're at it."

Yep, my ass hopped right down off that counter so damn fast it was a wonder I didn't face plant on the gray travertine floor. "Alrighty, then. Time to see another room." I grabbed her hand and tugged her into the formal living room, shifting uncomfortably as my jeans became just a little too tight.

And then there we were, in another room I didn't spend much time in. After all, there wasn't a television, which meant I had limited interest in the space.

"I'm sensing a theme here, Sebastian."

"Yeah? What's that?"

"Did your decorator only see things in black and white?"

She sounded serious, but I was pretty sure she was joking.

"My stepmother deserves all the credit for the decorating. Even before she was married to Conrad, she…" I tried to think of a nicer way to say what was on my mind. "Let's just say Lauren's always been a part of Conrad's life. At least for as long as I can remember."

Lauren Trovato was a woman who went after what she wanted. And just like the saying went, nothing would stand in her way. Not even Conrad's previous wives.

But yeah, I got where Payton was coming from on the décor. It was right there in … well … in black and white. The two sofas were black leather, the side chair was white leather, and they were wrapped around a chrome-and-glass table that sat atop a plush black-and-white rug. The centerpiece for the room was the fireplace, which was shared between two rooms, fixed in a wall constructed of jagged natural quartz tiles stacked from floor to ceiling that separated the area from the formal dining room.

"It needs color, huh?"

"It needs something."

I pulled Payton to me until her breasts rubbed against my chest. I took both of her hands, linked our fingers together, and then pulled her arms behind her, holding them at the small of her back. The position left her fully at my mercy. "Right now, it's got everything I could possibly need."

Her cheeks turned a lovely shade of pink, and she licked her lips, making my dick throb. God, this woman was unraveling me.

"Well, what do you say we add this room to the list?" Payton's raspy tone held a seductive note that wasn't doing anything to quench the lust surging through my veins.

"What list?" I dared to ask.

"The list of rooms we christen later."

Oh, hell. A loud rumble came from my chest as I leaned down and pressed my mouth to hers, pulling her more tightly against me, trying to refrain from laying her out right there on the couch. "Angel, you're tempting a very hungry man right now."

Payton's answer to that was a smile that sent a shockwave through me, similar to a direct hit from a lightning strike.

"Next room," I mumbled against her lips, not wanting to release her just yet.

Unable to resist, I thrust my tongue into her mouth, licking her tongue, tasting her sweetness. When I did pull away, her face was flushed and her chest was rising and falling rapidly, similar to mine. To see her reaction to me, it was as much of an aphrodisiac as kissing her.

Knowing we were playing with fire, I led her to the next room.

"Do you actually eat in here?" Payton asked, pulling me to a stop when I would have just kept going. I'd been wrong earlier when I'd said I spent the least amount of time in the kitchen. Truth was, I rarely stepped foot in the dining room, and I knew for a fact, in the seven years that I'd lived in that house, not once had I eaten at that table.

"Not once," I answered and kept moving.

I led her down a narrow hallway to two guest rooms with elaborate baths attached. Prior to my impromptu plan to move, I had intended for Leif to move into one of the guest rooms while the other would continue to go untouched. Truth was, I had used those rooms on occasion, but only when I brought a woman back to my place. I'd never taken a woman to my bedroom, preferring something a little less personal. Needless to say, I wouldn't be using either of those rooms tonight. If Payton was going to be in bed with me, we were going to be in my bed.

"Want to see the room I spend the most time in?" I asked her, purposely lowering my voice.

She blushed and nodded.

I knew what she was thinking, but I didn't bother to tell her that she was wrong. The room she was thinking about was actually upstairs, which I did spend a fair amount of time in, if sleeping counted. She trailed behind me, still holding both of my hands, which I had behind my back. We had to detour back through the dining room, then the living room, and once again the kitchen before heading down a wide hallway.

I took her through a set of industrial glass doors and outside onto the patio surrounding the massive pool.

"This isn't a room," Payton told me, squeezing my hand.

"Nope, it's a pool."

"And this is where you spend most of your time?"

"Nope," I answered honestly. "That would be where I spend most of my time." I nodded toward a separate structure that housed my workout room. It was technically a guesthouse — I know … a guesthouse at the guesthouse. A little pretentious, but what did you expect from Conrad?

"What is it?" Payton asked.

"Workout room." I led her to the far end of the pool, punched in a key code, and slid open the glass door so she could see inside. The open space was relatively empty except for a heavy bag hanging from the ceiling, a treadmill in one corner, and a wall of free weights sitting in perfect, obsessive-compulsive order on one side. I nodded my head to the opposite end of the room. "There's a kitchen on that side, and a bathroom, complete with sauna, on the other end."

"I can see why you're in here so much. If it were my place, I'd probably sleep out here."

"The floor's a little hard, but likely doable," I told her as I stepped up behind her and licked the outer shell of her ear.

Payton shuddered and my body tensed yet again.

By the end of the night — or morning, considering it was already closing in on two o'clock — I would likely need to dunk myself in that pool regardless of how fucking cold it was.

Because I had been right earlier … I was definitely playing with fire.

Chapter Seven

Payton

I knew that Conrad Trovato was loaded. After all, I worked for the man, I saw the way he dressed, the car that he drove. Hell, I'd even been to his house.

So, it was only logical that I'd considered the fact that Sebastian might be wealthy, as well. He had informed me that Conrad was his father, which made the assumption relative.

However, after seeing his house, I was starting to wonder just what kind of money these people really had.

The guesthouse had a guesthouse. I mean, really. Come on now.

But rather than trying to determine Sebastian's net worth, I was really interested in the first question I'd had when we'd driven through the main gates of Conrad's estate a short while ago. Why did Sebastian live on his father's estate?

My initial surprise had come when we'd passed the well-lit main house before heading down a winding road that led to this secondary house. It was then that I realized where we were. It just didn't make sense to me that Sebastian would live so close. Especially considering their volatile relationship. As much as I wanted to know why that was, that wasn't something I was going to ask him at the moment. The last thing I had on my agenda for the night was to bring up Conrad. I preferred to enjoy my time with Sebastian, not cast a black cloud over it by bringing up a sore subject.

Up to this point, I'd just been enjoying our time together, watching him, listening to his voice. My entire focus had been on him.

Well, that was until I started feeling a little uneasy about where he lived. Not that I cared about the money. In fact, I was having the opposite reaction, I think. I was a little intimidated, not at all comfortable around this kind of wealth.

I was more of a pizza-and-beer type of girl. I certainly wasn't a fan of champagne and caviar. Not that Sebastian seemed the type, either, but I knew very little about the lifestyle of the rich and famous. My thoughts drifted back to the party I'd attended last weekend, the overdressed socialites who'd been present, the long list of people who worked for Mr. Trovato, including the butler. It was awkward to be around that.

My parents weren't loaded. My father owned his own business, and they made a good living, but they were frugal with their money, and they'd passed that trait on to me. I certainly didn't make the sort of money to keep up with someone like Mr. Trovato — it'd probably take me a lifetime to make what Conrad brought home in a week.

And until seeing this place that Sebastian called home, I hadn't seen anything that would lead me to believe Sebastian was following in his father's footsteps in the finance department. But Sebastian's house looked like it came right out of a magazine, right down to the gleaming surfaces of everything in the place. What was worse was that it didn't look like anyone actually lived there and that … well, it kind of bothered me.

Truth was, I felt a little out of place. No, make that a lot out of place.

The only thing that helped to settle my anxiety was the fact that Sebastian didn't act like he had money. Or like he lived in a house that was probably the size of my entire apartment building.

Realizing that I was getting lost in my own thoughts again, I turned around to face Sebastian. "You gonna show me the rest?"

The heat in his golden gaze sent another tremor through my insides. I was so out of my element with this guy, but being with him just felt so right. It didn't matter if we were at my apartment, the racetrack, at IHOP sharing pancakes, or even here, in this ostentatiously decorated, cold place that Sebastian called home.

None of that mattered when he was with me.

"Not a lot left to see," he replied, his voice rougher than before. His eyes were raking over my face, briefly pausing on my mouth, and I could feel my breaths coming in more rapidly.

"You have to sleep somewhere," I whispered.

"Upstairs. Bedroom. Not much to see there," he said in a rush.

This was what we'd been dancing around since we'd arrived. The whole reason we'd spent the last half hour taking a tour of his house. Sebastian was avoiding the inevitable, and I knew he was giving me an out. As much as I loved him for that, I didn't want an out. I was burning alive, eager to be with this man. I wanted to spend the night in his arms, curled up against his body. But first, I wanted to feel him. To feel his naked body pressed against mine while he slid deep inside me.

Another shudder racked my body, and I knew it had nothing to do with the relatively chilly night air blowing in through the open glass door.

Knowing he wasn't going to say anything more, I slid my hands up Sebastian's hard chest, feeling the flex of his muscles beneath my palms, observing the heavy rise and fall as his breathing quickened, watching his face as his eyes studied me. "Show me your bedroom, Sebastian."

I was astounded by my own forwardness but not enough to care. Having spent the last few hours with him, the subtle teases, the mind-blowing kisses, they'd turned me into an inferno of desire, and I wasn't sure I was going to last much longer.

Sebastian's eyes locked with mine, and I didn't break the contact, willing him to read my mind, to know just what I was thinking.

I was ready for this.

More than ready.

As though he heard the unspoken words, Sebastian nodded, sliding his hands down my back and cupping my butt firmly before pulling me flush against him. His erection pressed into my belly, and I was suddenly anxious to see him naked, to admire all of him. "I want this, Sebastian," I assured him.

Another nod and then I was following him back into the house. He flipped off the lights as we made our way through each of the downstairs rooms. He paused once more when we ended up at the bottom of a beautiful half-spiral staircase that led to the second floor.

For a brief second, I thought I was going to have to take the lead, but then we were moving again. Sebastian's fingers tightened on mine as we took each step. When we reached the second floor, I realized instantly that this was where he spent most of his time. At least when he wasn't working out.

The space was open and airy with high vaulted ceilings, two oversized ceiling fans dangling above, and a wall of solid windows on the far end. I couldn't tell what was beyond the glass because there was nothing but darkness on the other side. I hadn't noticed when we were downstairs, but a half wall offered a view of the main living area below. There was a giant flat-screen television mounted on one wall above a sophisticated, modern fireplace.

Aside from two oversized leather recliners, there was a black sofa that lined the half wall and faced the television. A black-and-white rug with giant circular patterns covered a large portion of the hardwood floor.

"Well, at least now I know," I said, trying to fight my nerves.

"Know what?" Sebastian asked, placing his hand on the small of my back as we walked through the room.

"That the color wasn't hiding up here."

Sebastian's sexy chuckle eased me somewhat.

And then my body stiffened when he placed his hand on the doorknob that led to the only other room upstairs.

When he pushed the door open, I went inside first and smiled.

"This is more like it," I said, not meaning to say the words aloud.

His bed was unmade, the bright white comforter haphazardly twisted as though he had just climbed out of bed. There was a bottle of water on the nightstand, and the television remote was lying on the rumpled sheets. "At least I'm not the only one who doesn't make my bed every day."

Although I was trying to lighten the mood, the tension was thick because we both knew exactly why we were there.

The door clicked when Sebastian closed it behind him, and my heart skipped a beat. I was nervous, but it wasn't a bad nervous. I wasn't having second thoughts or doubts of any kind. I was just…

I didn't have time to complete that thought because Sebastian was stalking toward me, his gaze intense and incredibly sexy. And just like that, the world disappeared, and the only thing in my universe was Sebastian Trovato.

His strong hands gripped my hips as his mouth brushed against mine. Not wanting to waste another second, I reached for the hem of his T-shirt, slowly lifting it up until I'd revealed the delicious golden skin beneath. His hand disappeared from my hip, but not for long. He reached behind his head and grabbed a handful of cotton, then easily pulled his shirt over his head and tossed it onto a nearby chair.

I took a moment to drink him in, my eyes sliding along the intricate lines of his tattoos, the hard ridges of muscle that made up his chest, the rippling edges of his abs. When he put his hand back on my hip, I saw his biceps flex as he gripped me tighter.

"Angel."

His voice was rough, sexy. As though he was just as affected by this as I was.

Placing my palms flat against his skin, I slid them up to his collarbone, then higher, over the thick muscles of his shoulders. I continued to touch him, memorizing every glorious inch of him until my fingernails were gently scraping the back of his head, letting his short hair tease my fingers.

To my relief, Sebastian's hands moved upward, beneath my T-shirt, warming my back. And the next thing I knew, my shirt was being discarded with his.

"Fuck," he breathed out. "You're … so damn beautiful." His words were raspy and rough, the admiration in his tone sending chills snaking down my spine.

This was seduction, pure and simple. There was no rush as we both took the time to enjoy what we saw. The way Sebastian's eyes flared when he looked at me gave me a strange sense of feminine power. No man had ever looked at me like that. Never had anyone taken the time to seduce me thoroughly, and I was pretty sure that no other moment in my life would live up to this one.

Sebastian walked me backward until my legs hit the edge of the bed. One of his hands slid behind me, bracing my back as he lowered me down, his other hand on the mattress so that he didn't come down on top of me. As I lay there, looking up at him, I knew that when I eventually went back to my normal life, I was not going to be the same person I was right then.

I'd already fallen a little bit in love with him, and I was sure that, by the time the sun came up over the horizon, I was going to be in deep. Deeper than I'd ever imagined possible.

"Payton." The way he said my name had my insides quivering. The way he looked at me, as though I were the only important thing in the world, had another wave of desire crashing through me.

I reached for him then, catching him off guard and pulling him down on top of me. His knee slid between my legs, grinding against my sex, making me crazy with lust, wishing like hell that we didn't have the rest of our clothes between us.

When his mouth met mine, I gave in to his kiss, meeting his tongue, sliding against it slowly. Although the tension was ratcheting up several notches, he was still going slowly. I wanted to beg him to hurry because I wasn't sure I could stand much more. I needed to feel him against me, the rough pads of his fingers on my skin, the gentle scrape of his scruffy jaw against my…

"Oh, God." The words slipped out as Sebastian's mouth traveled down to my breast; the delicious rasp of his tongue against my oversensitive flesh had my body bowing into him.

A flutter of sensation erupted in my core when he slid my bra out of the way and took my nipple into his mouth. Warmth flooded me, causing my eyes to close, my body to tingle. The sensual torture continued for long seconds, and then he was trailing back up to my mouth.

His kiss turned hungry, desperate, and I met him with a fury of my own. Feeling bold, I slid my hands down between our bodies, the tips of my fingers sliding into the waistband of his jeans before I deftly unhooked the button and lowered the zipper.

Sebastian's lips brutally assaulted mine, making me moan into his mouth as I slid my hands into his jeans and boxers, finding his steel-hard length and stroking him slowly. The growl that erupted from his chest spurred me on. I maintained a slow, steady pace, eager but not wanting to rush this. I wanted to touch him, to taste him.

"Payton." Sebastian's breath was heaving in and out of his lungs as he pulled back, staring down at me. His eyes were a little wild, and I imagined I looked much the same. "Angel. Oh, damn, that feels good."

The guttural sound of his voice only intensified the ache that had started between my thighs. I was grinding myself against his leg, trying to ease the desperate need but failing.

"Your hands are so fucking soft," he mumbled, his mouth hovering over mine but not touching. His forehead rested against mine, as though he didn't have the strength to hold himself up. I didn't stop, enjoying the smooth, velvety length of him in my hands. His hips thrust forward a few times, followed by more growls.

And I knew then that I might not survive the night, but heaven help me, it was going to be so worth it.

Chapter Eight

Sebastian

Payton's hands were like silk. She was so tentative with her touch I was surprised I could breathe. The woman was going to kill me little by little, and I couldn't think of a better way to go.

I was trying to be gentle, unhurried, not wanting to overwhelm her, but I wanted to lick my way up her body. Slowly. So that I could drive her as crazy as I was. And yet she was the one holding the reins, controlling everything from my respiration to my thoughts.

"Payton," I rasped, hardly able to get her name out of my mouth. As it was, I was resting my forehead against hers as the pleasure overwhelmed me. I never wanted her to stop stroking me, but if I didn't do something, I was going to be the only one at the finish line, and I wasn't ready for the race to be over just yet.

Somehow — don't ask me how — I managed to get my brain to function, to send instructions to my hands to get them moving. Gripping her wrists, I succeeded in halting her mind-blowing movements. She didn't release my cock, though, causing me to gasp for air as she teased the tip with her thumb and making me sweat as she did.

"If you only knew how good that felt," I told her, inhaling deeply. "But unless you want me to finish now, you're gonna have to release me."

Her smile lit up her face, her bright yellow-green eyes glowing in the dim light cast by the bedside lamp. God, the woman was so fucking beautiful when she smiled. She was beautiful anyway, but when she smiled, she was otherworldly.

Finding a minimal amount of strength within me, I managed to push myself up off the bed, sliding my hand down the center of her body as I got to my feet. Down her neck, her chest, between her luscious breasts, and then down her flat belly, I stopped at the button of her jeans. Watching her face, I slowly unhooked the button. The only sounds I heard were my own heartbeat pounding in my ears and the combined rasp of our rapid breaths. Her chest expanded as I lowered the zipper, the metal teeth releasing one at a time. Leaning forward, I pressed my lips to her stomach, sliding my tongue into her navel as I pushed the denim down over her hips, revealing a pair of silky black panties that matched the bra she was still wearing.

As I pushed her jeans down her trim thighs, she moved, slipping her shoes off and letting them land with a gentle thud on the hardwood.

"So fucking beautiful," I muttered, the words but a mere whisper as I stared at her in awe. Her skin was so smooth, so soft, and I couldn't resist touching her, not wanting to stop.

Ever.

Once her jeans were discarded, I hurried out of my own, keeping my eyes on her the entire time. I couldn't turn away, even if I had wanted to. Which I damn sure didn't.

Not wanting to rush, I left my boxers on, but before I could join her on the bed, Payton surprised me yet again by sitting up, her legs dangling over the side.

I thought for a moment that I was going to swallow my fucking tongue.

She was sitting on the edge of the bed, her legs spread while I stood inches from her. Her lips pressed against my stomach, her tongue gliding against my skin. I slid my hands into her hair, holding her. I told myself it was so I could stop her, to keep her from doing something that would blow my world to pieces, but I knew better.

I wasn't strong enough to resist her.

Her hand slid up my thigh, beneath my boxers, and when she cupped me, I damn near came right then and there. Her touch was so gentle, almost reverent, and I swear, in all my life, I'd never felt anything as good as Payton's hands on me.

And when she lowered my boxers, freeing me completely, the grip I had on her hair tightened.

Her sharp inhale had me looking down as she wrapped her fingers around my length. She was looking up at me, still smiling, a sexy, mischievous gleam in her eyes that had my body throbbing. Every ounce of blood I had made an immediate detour to my cock.

"Payton." I knew what she was going to do. She was going to make me lose it, but I was powerless to stop her. When her eyes left mine, her soft hand stroked me once, twice, and then her mouth was on me. "Oh, fuck. Payton. Baby. Angel. Oh, God, yes."

Yes, I knew I was rambling, but my brain cells were obliterated when she wrapped her lips around me. She was so gentle I wanted to beg her to take me deeper, to suck me harder, but I was scared I would freak her out. Her tentativeness, her hesitancy, spoke of inexperience. Part of me was thrilled with the idea that Payton might not have been with another man before, the other part wasn't sure she could handle me.

The beast that lived and breathed inside of me was clawing to get out. I wanted to climb on top of her and drive myself deep inside her body, pounding into her until she was screaming my name, her body gripping mine. It was all I'd thought about for the last few days, and here we were. By the grace of God, I was managing to hold back.

Barely.

I gripped her hair tightly and pulled her head back. I couldn't handle much more. She was going to send me over the edge far too soon if she kept doing that. When she looked up at me, I noticed her eyes were glazed, her pretty pink lips swollen.

Someone was testing me. That was all there was to it.

"My turn," I told her as I released her hair, sliding my hand down her back and deftly unhooking her bra before pulling it from her body and tossing it with the rest of our clothes. "Lie back," I instructed, and when she did, I slipped her panties down her legs.

And nearly had a heart attack.

She waxed.

Yep, there was no doubt about it, someone was testing me.

I was pretty sure I was going to fail the test, but I really didn't give a shit at that point.

While I locked my gaze with hers, I kicked off my boxers, then lowered myself to my knees on the floor beside the bed, my shoulders forcing her legs wider, opening her to me.

"Sebastian." My name on her lips sounded very much like a warning, but I didn't heed it. I leaned forward and took her in my mouth, kissing her tenderly, softly, using my fingers to separate the soft, slick folds of her sex. Similar to the way she'd handled me. And when she was writhing on the bed, her hands clutching the comforter beneath her, I continued to torment her with gentle licks, firm flicks of my tongue, until she shattered.

I knew I wasn't going to last much longer. Not this first time. As much as I wanted to spend the rest of the night getting her off with my mouth, I knew I wasn't going to last.

I made it to my feet, admiring the way she looked, a soft sheen on her skin, her eyes hooded as she peered up at me. I gave her a moment while I retrieved a condom from the nightstand drawer and rolled it on. When I looked up, I saw that she was watching me, and I knew it was time. I had to have her. I couldn't wait any longer. I crawled over her, forcing her to move farther up on the bed until her head rested on my pillow, her dark hair fanning out around her beautiful, flushed face.

"I've wanted this since the very first time I laid eyes on you," I told her, nuzzling her neck, sliding my tongue over her skin. "I've wanted to bury myself inside you, feel you gripping me…"

When her arms wrapped around me, her nails digging into my back ever so slightly, my body hardened even more than I thought possible. I trailed kisses along her jaw, then met her mouth with mine, plunging my tongue inside, letting her taste herself on my lips. She moaned, the sound so fucking perfect I wanted to make her do it again and again.

Easing between her legs, I rested on my forearm, reaching between us and guiding myself to her entrance. Her breath hitched when I slid into her, her head pressing into the pillow.

I paused, not daring to go any deeper. "I don't want to hurt you, Angel."

Payton opened her eyes and met my stare. "You won't hurt me," she said, and she sounded so sure of herself I slid forward slowly, sinking into her.

"Angel." I could barely speak, my lungs seizing up from the sheer ecstasy of her body contracting, pulling me deeper.

"Sebastian."

I stilled, watching her. The emotions that fluttered over her face had my heart pounding harder. Thank God I wasn't the only one feeling this. Whatever it was, it was stronger than anything I'd ever felt. And I damn sure wasn't the type to confuse sex with love. But this wasn't just sex. The only way I knew that was because this felt unlike anything I'd ever known before.

I kept myself propped on one forearm, sliding my other hand down her body and cupping her thigh, pulling her leg up and opening her more as I slid deeper. Impossibly deep.

Our eyes met, locked, held. I didn't look away. As the overwhelming pleasure accosted me, I peered into Payton's eyes and she into mine. I was baring my soul to this woman, and I was pretty sure she realized that. Her hands gripped my back, her fingernails scraping my skin. It was a sensual torture that had chills racing down my body.

"I don't know how long I can do this," I told her.

"Do what?" she asked, breathless, a small smile tipping the very corners of her mouth.

"Go slow. It's … killing me. You're… Oh, damn, Payton. You unhinge me." I smiled, despite the pleasure-pain that was building to a crescendo as I continued to penetrate her, easing in deep, withdrawing slowly.

"I don't want slow," she said, her smile luminous.

When she slid her hands down my back and grabbed my ass, pulling me to her, the last of my restraint dissolved.

And as I made love to Payton, driving into her, faster, harder, until she was crying out my name, begging me to make her come, I knew that I would go to the ends of the earth for this woman.

She owned me.

And no one … absolutely no one would ever keep her from me.

Chapter Nine

Payton

Sunday morning

Sebastian's bedroom was dark, the heavy shades pulled over the window blocking out the early-morning sun. As I lay there, my head resting on Sebastian's chest, his fingers trailing softly up and down my spine, I knew I should have given in to my exhaustion, but going to sleep seemed like a waste of the moment. Even there in his arms, with his warmth wrapped around me, I had no desire to leave him, even just to sleep.

"What're you thinking about?" he whispered, kissing my forehead, the stubble along his jaw gently scraping my skin, reminding me of what we'd just done.

"You," I admitted truthfully. Fact was, I was always thinking about him.

His body tensed slightly, and I ran my palm over his abs, feeling the muscles tighten. There was so much I knew about him, mostly how his body felt inside me, how his breaths rushed hard and fast when he came, how he growled out my name when his climax overtook him, and the incredible scent of his skin. But there was still so much I didn't know. So much I wanted to know. Realizing that the timing might never be right to ask the difficult questions, I went with my gut, deciding to go for it.

"Why do you keep it a secret that you're Conrad's son?" I asked, keeping my tone soft, even.

"It's not a secret I keep," he informed me, his voice carrying an edge of frustration.

"Why does Conrad keep it a secret?" My mind drifted back to the mental images I had of Conrad's office. There weren't any pictures of Sebastian in there. Only ones of Aaliyah growing up, a few of Conrad's wife, but none of Sebastian. My heart clenched painfully in my chest.

"I didn't know who my father was until I was fourteen years old," he explained, his tone sounding far away. "The year my mother died."

My stomach ached from his admission, and I suddenly regretted my decision to bring it up. He sounded so lost. While my mind tried to piece together just what that meant, my heart hurt for a little boy who'd lost his mother and been thrust into a world he wasn't familiar with. He hadn't known his father? I didn't say anything, just curled up tightly against Sebastian, hoping he would continue.

"I had two choices when she died. Go live with a man I didn't know, or take my chances in foster care."

"There wasn't anyone else? What about your mother's parents?"

"I didn't know my grandparents. They disowned my mother before I was born. She was a senior in high school when she got pregnant with me. When she refused to get an abortion, they threw her out of their house."

Oh, my God.

"From what she told me, from the stories my aunt shared, they were God-fearing people. A bastard child was unacceptable in their world, something that would be frowned upon by those they knew. They weren't willing to endure the wrath of God for my mother's sins."

I bit my tongue, not wanting to interrupt Sebastian's story, but I was suddenly worried I wouldn't be able to handle the horror of what it had been like for him growing up. I had two parents who had doted on me. My grandparents, both paternal and maternal, had been wonderful, loving people who never judged anyone. My grandmother on my father's side was the only one still alive, the others having passed through the years from old age and natural causes. I still visited my grandmother although she didn't really know who I was anymore. The benefit was that I still got to see her. And above all else, I still had so many incredible memories of my childhood.

"The only person who helped my mother was my mother's only sister, Tina. But even she couldn't do much. And when my mother died, Tina had been in and out of drug rehab for several years, and according to the courts, she wasn't equipped to handle a rebellious teenager. I took my chances with Conrad."

"How did your mother die?" I asked, swallowing hard as I waited for his answer.

Again, Sebastian's body tightened, his breath hitching in his chest. I clung to him, hoping he would continue, worried he wouldn't.

Several minutes passed before Sebastian spoke again. "My mother died in a car accident. She was T-boned on her way home from work one night. She'd recently started a second job, waitressing at a different restaurant, working the late shift. That night, she never came home."

Doing the math in my head, I knew that Aaliyah had to be relatively close to Sebastian in age, and that meant... I couldn't bring myself to ask the question that hovered on the tip of my tongue. I wasn't sure I wanted to know whether his stepmother had been there for Sebastian, taking him in and trying to fill the hole that would have been left within him when his mother died. Instead, I said, "Tell me about your mom."

Sebastian sighed, his arm tightening around me. "She was fun. We didn't have much, but she always made sure that what we lacked in material possessions, she made up for in the time we spent together. It was always just the two of us.

"When I was born, Conrad tried to pay her off, refusing to be part of my life. He was married at the time." Sebastian paused, his chest rising with his deep inhale. "Twenty-six years old and married to his first wife. My mother was seventeen when she had me."

I tried not to show my shock, but when Sebastian's lips brushed the top of my head, I knew I had failed.

"He tried to buy her silence. At first he tried to pay her to have an abortion. She refused him the same way she refused her parents. And when I was born, he tried to pay her off to keep her quiet." Sebastian paused again. "My mother loved him. She loved him, and I don't think she ever stopped. Maybe she should've taken the money…"

"It sounds like she was a strong woman. She did what she thought was best for you."

"She was great. She was my best friend. But I wasn't the best kid. As I got older, I started hanging with the wrong crowd. By the time I was thirteen, I'd been arrested several times. Most of the time for stupid shit. Petty theft, street racing. I hated going home because, as the years passed, the light in her eyes continued to dim.

"I remember her mentioning to me that she was gonna try to get in touch with my father. We were flat broke, and I'd started working for cash at a local mechanic shop to help out. She hated that I had to work to try to help out. She was working two jobs, waitressing at two different places. But it wasn't enough."

"Did she get in touch with him?" I asked, knowing the answer before he responded.

"If she did, she didn't tell me. She tried to shelter me from that shit. I remember her always pretending that we had more than we did, but I knew. I knew when I looked in the refrigerator that the only thing I would find was a jug of water, sometimes milk. I knew that when I woke up to go to school, she'd be dead on her feet in the kitchen, pouring what little milk we had into a bowl or pulling bread out of the toaster for my breakfast. And I knew when I finally decided to come home after school, she'd be going to her second job."

"But Conrad took you in when she died?" I asked, hating how that sounded.

"Not willingly," Sebastian said, his tone reflecting the anger I'd sensed in him yesterday when he'd showed up at my apartment.

I lifted my head, peering at him in the darkness, waiting for him to explain.

"I'm not a saint, Payton," he whispered. "You should know that now."

I was surprised by his admission, but I didn't know what it meant. What he said next was not what I expected to hear.

He moved, effectively coming over me as I rolled to my back.

"But I swear to you, Angel," he whispered, his voice dark and dangerous, "I'll never hurt you. I'll never let anyone hurt you."

His words sounded like a warning, like he was telling me something, but I just didn't know what. I could hardly make out his features in the dark, but I could see enough that I knew the anger was back. I wanted that anger to go away, to disappear entirely. Placing my hands on his face, I forced a smile I didn't feel. "I believe you, Sebastian."

His eyes flared briefly and then his lips were on mine. I knew the conversation was over. At least for now. And when he positioned himself over me, reaching for a condom on the bedside table, I didn't try to stop him. And when he finally slid inside me, I wrapped my arms around him, nuzzled my face in his neck, and held him as close as I could.

This man ... he wasn't the only one unhinged. I sensed the darkness and the danger that lurked inside him, but it didn't scare me. In fact, I felt just the opposite. I was drawn to him. So much so that I knew my life was irrevocably changed from that moment forward.

After all ... I loved him.

Two hours later, I awoke alone in Sebastian's bed, tangled in the expensive sheets. A quick glance around his still-darkened bedroom told me he wasn't there. Forcing myself out of his bed, I ignored the sweet ache between my thighs that reminded me of the last few hours. I grabbed his black T-shirt from the chair and pulled it on over my head. I didn't even bother to try and find a mirror, knowing that I was a mess.

Something told me that I needed to find Sebastian.

When I walked out of his bedroom, the bright light of day filled the house, momentarily blinding me with its intensity. There weren't any window coverings to block out the natural light that filled the space. I waited a moment for my eyes to adjust, and then I went in search of Sebastian. When I didn't find him downstairs, I headed outside, my feet carrying me to the separate building. That was where he'd said he spent most of his time, so it seemed like the logical place to look.

I found him in his workout room. The sliding glass door was open, and he was whaling away on the heavy bag hanging from the ceiling, music blaring loudly. I recognized the song — "Not Falling" by Mudvayne — which made me smile. We had similar taste in music.

He didn't seem to notice me at first, and I didn't announce myself, content to watch him as I leaned against the doorframe. The way his muscles flexed and bunched as he moved. He was pure masculine grace.

He was wearing jeans but nothing else. I took him in from his bare feet, up over his thick legs, his washboard abs contracting with every jab… I was just getting to his chest when he moved, turning completely away from me.

The air in my lungs escaped as if I were the one punching that bag.

The tattoo…

Holy crap.

The tattoo that covered his back left me momentarily speechless. He had mentioned that he had a cross on his back, but that… Yeah, that was so much more than a cross. What caught my eye was the angel wings that spanned the entire width of his back, surrounding the cross. It was … breathtaking.

I didn't move, didn't breathe as I watched his body shift with so much precision it made my mouth dry. The tattoo shifted over his muscles, the wings seeming to move as he did.

I don't know if he knew I was there or if he was just stopping because he was tired, but all of a sudden, he wasn't moving, his hands gripping the heavy bag, the muscles in his shoulders tense. When he turned to face me, I realized he had to have known I was there. How, I don't know. It wasn't like he could have heard me over the sound of the music pulsing through the room.

His chest glistened with sweat, his hair disheveled, his eyes wide as he looked back at me. Without thinking, I moved to him, unable to stay away. He took three steps, closing the gap between us. The next thing I knew, Sebastian had lifted me, my legs wrapping around his hips as he moved to the wall, using the hard surface to support my weight as he crushed his mouth to mine. I twined my fingers in his hair, pulling. I don't know what came over me, but whatever it was, I was powerless to resist even if I had wanted to.

Which I didn't.

The song changed, but the tempo did not. The music was fast, almost angry, the bass thumping to match the sound of my pounding heart. I didn't release him, my hands sliding down his back, digging into his flesh as he pressed me into the wall.

He was breathing hard, the kiss stealing what was left of the oxygen in the room.

His arm moved, sliding down between us, and that was when I realized he was unfastening his jeans. He pulled back, our eyes meeting, and the unsaid question hung between us. Unless he had a condom in his pocket, we were without protection, but still I wanted him. Maybe more now than ever.

"I'm on the pill," I said in a rush. I let the silence linger between us briefly, waiting for him to speak.

"Payton—"

I cut him off by slamming my mouth to his. I trusted him. I trusted him implicitly, and I didn't need to hear anymore.

"Now, Sebastian," I urged, nipping his lower lip beside his lip ring. "I need you inside me now."

What came next could be described as nothing more than pure, unadulterated fucking. It was extreme, and although we were using one another as a release, there was so much more to it. So much more that bubbled just beneath the surface.

Sebastian shifted, and then he was slamming inside me, my breath lodged in my throat with the first gloriously brutal thrust of his hips.

"Angel," he breathed against my ear. "I need you."

78

"I'm here." I would always be there. I didn't tell him as much, but there was something between us. A connection, a bond that was stronger than anything I'd ever felt, and words weren't necessary.

"Harder," I pleaded, my fingernails digging into his skin.

Sebastian didn't hold back. He was pounding into me, driving me higher and higher until there was no holding back. The friction … the wonderful feeling of him inside me was too much. My orgasm crested, and I shattered right there in his arms, pressed up against the wall. The roar that followed signaled Sebastian's release, and the grip he had on me intensified until I wasn't sure I could breathe from how tight he was holding me. It didn't stop me from pulling him closer, crushing him to me.

It was then that I knew… Whatever this was between us, it was so powerful, so potent, there was no way that either of us would survive it intact.

Chapter Ten

Payton
Sunday evening

"Well, it's about time, kiddo," my father greeted me when I walked in the front door of my parents' house at five thirty. Harold Fowler, better known as Hal, got to his feet and came toward me, pulling me into a bear hug before Aaron even managed to close the door behind us.

"Women," Aaron muttered with a grin as he passed me, making his way to my father and reaching out to shake his hand. "It takes 'em forever to get ready."

Considering I'd come right home from Sebastian's, hopped in the shower, and pulled my wet hair up in a clip, I knew Aaron was talking out his ass. And likely trying to cover for me. Which I loved him for, by the way. I had threatened him within an inch of his life if he even mentioned to my parents that I was seeing someone. Although he had pestered me relentlessly, promising that was the first thing he was going to tell my father, I knew he wouldn't.

"Sometimes I think you might have the right idea, Aaron," Hal teased, and I nearly choked as I pulled off my jacket and tossed it on the back of the long sofa where my father had been sitting when we came in.

"Trust me, Dad," I said as I moved through the room, glaring at Aaron, "gay guys are incredibly high maintenance. Don't let him fool you."

Aaron's laugh was the last thing I heard as I slipped down the hall toward the kitchen.

"Mom?" I called as I stepped into the kitchen to find it deserted, despite the heavenly aroma that drifted through the open, airy room.

My parents still lived in the same house where I'd grown up. The décor had changed over the years, and they'd done quite a few upgrades here and there, but other than that, it still felt like home to me. A place I knew I could come whenever I needed comfort. Or food.

I needed food, but I probably would've just stayed at the apartment and snacked on popcorn if it hadn't been for the dinner invitation my father had issued on my voice mail. When he'd invited Aaron as well, I couldn't tell him no, so here we were.

"In here," my mother hollered back.

I turned to see her in the separate dining room, setting plates and silverware out on the table.

Susan Fowler was an incredibly beautiful woman, even when she was wearing a Dallas Stars sweatshirt, old ratty jeans, and an apron. Her short blond bob framed her face and made her appear years younger than she was. Not that she was old. But at forty-six, people often mistook her for my sister. My father insisted that I got my good looks from her, but in reality, I looked more like him. I had inherited his dark hair and hazel eyes, while I had gotten my height — or lack thereof — from my mother's side.

"It smells fantastic," I told my mother when she returned to the kitchen, pulling me to her for a quick hug. "What're we having?"

"Homemade chili," she replied with a giant grin. "And sweet cornbread."

My mother was an extraordinary cook, and she was always trying new things, which meant that there was probably some twist to this homemade chili, but I didn't doubt that it would be fabulous. If nothing else, I could probably survive off her sweet cornbread — she knew it was my favorite.

"I'm starving," I told her, pulling out a barstool and hopping onto it while I watched her move efficiently through the kitchen.

"Good. And I hope you brought Aaron, because I made enough to feed a small army."

"The army's here," Aaron said as he joined us. He made a beeline for my mother, hugging her tightly before sitting beside me at the breakfast bar.

"How's school?" Susan asked Aaron as she washed her hands in the sink in front of us.

"Oh, you know … boring," Aaron answered easily, gifting her with his infectious smile.

"Of course it is," she agreed before turning her attention to me. "How's work?"

She turned to the stove, reaching for a spoon to stir the pot as she glanced back over her shoulder at me.

"Great," I said. I didn't know what else I was supposed to say. "Oh, I'm going to Vegas on Tuesday."

My mother dropped the spoon onto the stovetop, jumping back to avoid the splatter from the chili. She reached for a hand towel while she stared at me. "What do you mean you're going to Vegas? With who?"

"My boss and his wife," I informed her, glancing over at Aaron, who looked just as surprised by my news. The gleam in his eyes promised retribution later. Apparently we hadn't talked much since I'd started seeing Sebastian, but in my defense, he had been pretty wrapped up in Mark until recently.

"For how long?" my mother asked, but before I could answer, she yelled at my father, telling him to join us in the kitchen.

I sighed. I knew I should have waited until dinner was over and I was getting ready to leave before I gave her the news.

"I'll be back sometime on Friday."

"What is this trip for?" My mother had stopped what she was doing to give me her full attention.

"The SEMA show," I told her as my father made an appearance around the wall.

"The SEMA show?" he asked, looking at me and then to my mother. "What about it?"

"It looks like your daughter will be going," she said, sounding not at all pleased by the news.

"With who?" he asked, his eyes narrowing on me.

"Mr. Trovato and his wife. I think their daughter may go with them."

"Where will you be staying?"

"Caesar's Palace."

"What will you be doing?"

My father's questions were rapid-fired at me, and I suddenly felt like I had when I had asked if I could go on a senior trip to Galveston. Glancing at Aaron, I smiled. "Does this sound at all familiar?"

"Little bit," he offered with a grin.

He had been on the receiving end of those questions back then, too, so at least he understood some of my pain.

Not that he tried to help run interference. He seemed quite content watching me squirm under their heated stares.

"I'm Conrad's assistant, Dad. I'll probably be taking notes, getting him coffee, making sure he knows where he's supposed to be." Truth was, I really didn't know what I would be doing while I was there. I'd been just as shocked as my parents were now when Conrad had insisted that I attend.

"The SEMA show is a trade show, Payton. Giant rooms full of people showing their skills and trades. It's all about cars and trucks. I'm just not sure I understand why you need to be there."

I sighed.

"Let's take this to the dinner table," my mother instructed, placing oven mitts over her slender hands and carrying the pot of chili to the dining room table.

I hopped off the barstool and resigned myself to having to deal with getting the third degree from my parents for the next half hour. I knew I should have just kept my mouth shut.

Half an hour turned into an hour and a half. By the time Aaron and I climbed into his Honda to make the short drive back to our apartment, I had been officially grilled and then grilled some more.

"They took that well," Aaron said facetiously, his chuckle reverberating through the car.

I sighed and pressed my head against the seat, staring out the window into the night. I already missed Sebastian. I hadn't been away from him for long, but I couldn't stop thinking about him. We had spent the entire day together, and I'd been reluctant to go home but hadn't wanted to overstay my welcome, either. When it'd become clear that he wasn't going to ask me to leave, I had found the courage to request it myself. Not because I had wanted to but because it was necessary.

"They'll be fine," I told Aaron. "I guess it's a good thing I didn't mention I was dating Conrad's son."

Aaron's head snapped toward me as if his neck were made of rubber. "His son?"

Well, apparently there was something else I hadn't told my best friend. "Yeah. His son."

"And you didn't know this?"

"Nope." I tried to sound casual, but it really was a big deal. Even I realized that. After all, I worked for Conrad. He signed my paychecks, and clearly he didn't have a good relationship with his son if they managed to keep the fact that they were related out of the press. It still stunned me how they had managed to do that, considering how high profile Conrad was in our area. Even my father, someone who kept up with everything that had to do with the automotive industry, didn't know that Conrad had a son. He had mentioned a rumor that he'd heard, but even he had dismissed the notion.

"Holy crap, Payton. That's... Wow. I don't even know what that is. What does Conrad think about you dating Sebastian?"

I turned my head to look at Aaron and raised my eyebrows. "He doesn't know."

"How would he not know that his assistant is dating his son?"

That was the question of the hour. One I couldn't answer, either.

I must've stunned Aaron with my revelation, because he was quiet for the remainder of the drive, and it wasn't until we walked into the house to find Toby and Chloe sitting on the couch watching a movie that he said something.

"Payton's dating Conrad Trovato's son."

Chloe's eyes widened and she clicked the mute button on the television. Toby looked like he'd just stepped into the twilight zone. Of course, being that he was Sebastian's friend, he would already know this.

"Sebastian is your boss's son?" she asked, sounding almost hysterical.

Sure, I thought it was a big deal, but not *that* big of a deal. I shrugged, said a quick hello to Toby, and then escaped to my bedroom.

I should have known that Chloe would follow me. Less than a minute later, she was flopping onto my bed and staring at me as I began rummaging through my closet, trying to figure out what I would wear to the office tomorrow.

"His son?" she asked, her voice low. "Was that a secret or something? How could you think he was just a mechanic and he turns out to be Conrad's son?"

"No idea," I told her truthfully. "But I really don't wanna talk about it." I didn't want to talk *period*. I couldn't get my mind off Sebastian as it was. I was missing him fiercely, and we'd only been apart for a few hours. Ever since I'd brought up Vegas to my mother, I had been trying to figure out just how I was going to make it through the next five days without seeing him.

"Well, if he's related, does that mean he's going to Vegas?"

"He hasn't mentioned it," I replied, pulling out a black skirt and a black sweater and laying them on my desk for tomorrow. I would have to go with red shoes to add a little color, I thought to myself. And that thought led me back to Sebastian as well, remembering how much his house lacked color.

I sighed.

"Did you ask him?" Chloe's curiosity was apparently getting the best of her.

"Why would I do that?" I asked, turning to face her and propping my hands on my hips. "I don't talk about work with him."

"What do you talk about?" she retorted, a glimmer of frustration in her green eyes.

"I don't know," I answered.

"Hey, Chloe!" Aaron yelled from the other room. "I think your boyfriend's getting bored in here."

Chloe's face lit up, her smile dazzling as she mouthed the word boyfriend.

And just like that, I was off the hook.

I smiled back, unable not to. I loved seeing her so happy.

When she left my room, Chloe closed the door behind her, leaving me to my thoughts. I was still smiling at how happy she was when my cell phone chimed, signaling an incoming text. I figured it was my mother, still wanting to talk about my upcoming trip.

I was tempted to ignore it, but the thought of it possibly being Sebastian had me lunging for my purse. When I pulled up my text app and saw the message, I slid to the floor, my smile weighing me down.

It was Sebastian.

And the text: *I miss you.*

Needless to say, I spent the rest of the evening thinking about him even more.

Chapter Eleven

Payton
Tuesday morning

The anxiety that I'd stored up about getting on an airplane was exacerbated by the fact that I was now on an airplane with Conrad, his wife, Lauren, and their daughter, Aaliyah. It didn't even matter that we were sitting in first class, being served champagne by a very attentive flight attendant who continued to smile at Aaliyah as though she'd hung the moon.

The champagne wasn't doing much for me, although I had downed it like water, spurred on by the minor panic attack I was currently having. Seeing that the man who was greeting each passenger with a huge smile and a pleasant good morning was more interested in Aaliyah wasn't helping to distract me nearly enough, either.

In her defense, I don't think Aaliyah even noticed that the young man serving us was practically drooling over her. And it wasn't because she was ignoring him or being in any way snooty. The woman seemed seriously oblivious to the number of heads she turned when she walked into a room — or on a plane, as was the case now.

The only positive in the whole screwed-up situation was that I was sitting in the first class section, beside Aaliyah on the back row, and her parents were sitting in the front row of seats, which put at least six people in between us. If I'd had to be any closer than that, I probably would've needed one of those oxygen masks to drop down from the ceiling.

"Relax," Aaliyah said kindly, patting the top of my hand where I was clutching the armrest as though the damn thing might just fly off my seat if I let go.

"Easier said than done," I told her, gritting my teeth as I spoke.

"It's gonna be fine," she assured me, but it didn't make me feel any better.

The captain had just informed us that we would be taking off soon and instructed the flight attendants to ready the cabin.

Closing my eyes, I pictured Sebastian, pulling up all of the images I could from the day we'd shared on Sunday. I hadn't seen him yesterday, not even after work, which had bothered me more than I was willing to admit. Although we had talked on the phone last night when I'd gotten home, not seeing him had been the wrinkle in my entire day.

Not that I had let him know that. I had tried to play it cool, not wanting to overwhelm him by asking that he come over. I was pretty sure that he would have, but I had stayed my ground and refused to make the request.

After spending the entire day with him on Sunday, swimming in his pool — which was heated, by the way — lounging in his Jacuzzi, and sharing three meals with him, I figured he might need a little time to recoup. I sure did, but that didn't mean that I wouldn't prefer to spend that time with him anyway.

When I'd informed him that I was going to Vegas with Conrad, he hadn't acted surprised. The brief "Be careful while you're there" that he'd offered wasn't much of a response, either.

"So, you're dating my brother, huh?" Aaliyah asked casually as she continued to flip through a magazine.

I turned my head to the side and peered over at her through one eye.

"What makes you say that?" I asked. I wasn't going to lie to her, but I did intend to feel her out a little before I divulged all of my secrets. Although I liked her immensely, I didn't know her all that well. Yet.

"That."

I had no idea what "that" meant, but I continued to focus my attention on her. She looked cool and collected, just as she always did. Her long blond hair was pulled back in a fancy up-do, her makeup was perfect, and her outfit reflected her immense wealth.

We were polar opposites. While I was short, Aaliyah was tall and willowy. She made me feel clumsy just sitting beside her. But she was so down-to-earth it was easy to overlook her beauty and class. Sort of. The fact that she was wearing a short turquoise dress that clung to every perfect curve had me wanting to hate her.

As for me, I was wearing jeans and an emerald-green sweater. Not dressy but not too casual. I had gone with heels rather than flats to add a little oomph to my outfit, but in no way did I resemble the blue-eyed debutante who had turned damn near every eye in the airport.

"What does 'that' mean?"

"The way your face turns just a little pink when he is mentioned. *He* being my brother."

I forced my gaze forward, feeling the warmth in my cheeks. "It does not," I countered without heat.

"It so does." Her laugh turned a few heads in the small section of the plane, including the attendant who gifted her with a wide grin.

The plane began its journey down the runway, gaining speed, and I clutched the armrests a little tighter. If I gripped them much harder, my fingers were going to break. I didn't open my eyes or release my death grip on the seat for a solid ten minutes and only then because Aaliyah nudged my shoulder. When I opened my eyes, it was to see a very helpful man was handing us a towel.

I glanced at Aaliyah, then at the passengers in front of us. What the hell was the towel for? Not wanting to look stupid, I reached for it and followed Aaliyah's lead, wiping my hands. Damn, that was hot. I tossed it between my hands, trying to force it to cool down a little, hoping no one noticed.

"He likes you, you know."

"Who?" I asked, glancing up at the attendant who was now walking away.

"Sebastian."

I jerked my attention back to her. "How do you know that?" I felt like a girl in high school, trying to find out if the boy I liked really liked me back. Although I wasn't the one who'd brought up the subject, I knew my eagerness for an answer was written all over my face.

"He's very protective of you."

I wasn't quite sure what Aaliyah was referring to, so I humored her. "How so?"

"When my father talks about you, Sebastian's ready to pounce."

The first part of that statement was what caught my attention. "Why does your father talk about me?"

"Oh, you know, normal dinner conversation."

Being the topic of Trovato dinner conversation didn't make me feel all that comfortable. I mean, sure, I got it … I worked for Conrad, but for him to discuss me over dinner… What the hell was there to talk about?

"If you wanna know the truth," Aaliyah said as she leaned closer to me, "I think he does it to piss Sebastian off."

That didn't sound all that fun. Why would Conrad do that?

I thought about the weekend I'd just spent with Sebastian … the things we'd done, the conversation we'd had. I knew if my mind drifted too far, my face would be beet-red. In order to avoid that, I turned back to Aaliyah. Letting my curiosity get the best of me, I changed the subject.

"How did your parents meet?" I knew the question was overly personal, especially to ask a woman I barely knew, but I wasn't interested in talking about Sebastian. I missed him already, and knowing that I was going to be away from him for the next few days was killing me.

"My mother used to work for him," Aaliyah said, closing her magazine and sliding it into the seat pocket in front of her. She pulled out the tray from the armrest of her seat, lowering it slowly in front of her and resting her clasped hands on the top.

She was so graceful, so sophisticated, it made me feel like a klutz. I pretended not to notice the vast differences between us.

When I had arrived at the airport, after making my way through security and locating my gate, I'd been a jumble of nerves and not just because I was about to get on a plane. But the moment Aaliyah had seen me, she had eased my nerves somewhat. She had approached quickly, giving me a brief hug and telling me to breathe. So, it had been obvious to her that I was starving my lungs for oxygen, too.

That was when I'd noticed the significant differences between Sebastian and Aaliyah. Considering they were half siblings, it was interesting to see that they didn't look much alike at all. In fact, aside from a few similar facial features like their nose and their cheekbones, the two of them looked nothing alike. Sebastian was tall, dark, and dangerous, while Aaliyah appeared sweet and innocent with her light hair and bright eyes.

"My mother was Conrad's assistant back in the very beginning."

"The beginning of what?" I asked, confused. Sebastian had told me that Lauren had been around for a long time, but I wanted more details.

"Back when he first started Trovato, Inc. She was his first assistant, and she remained with him for years. In fact, she worked for him up until he proposed."

I knew from my research and the minimal details Sebastian had offered that Lauren was Conrad's third wife. Which meant… "So, they've known each other for a long time," I said, unsure just how to voice what was really on my mind.

"Definitely," Aaliyah said confidently. "My mother was there when Conrad's first and second wives left him."

I wondered why they'd left. Did it have anything to do with Lauren? Or because Conrad was clearly unfaithful? Had he been unfaithful with Lauren, too? After all, he had been married to his first wife when he'd gotten Sebastian's mother pregnant.

Not that I was going to ask those questions — it seemed a little presumptuous to think that Lauren might've been the very reason Conrad's previous marriages hadn't worked out. I had no idea how old Lauren was, but if I had to guess, based on her looks, she was several years younger than Conrad. That or she had an incredible plastic surgeon.

Truth was, I didn't think Lauren liked me all that much. I had only spoken to her on the phone until that morning when I had met them at the airport. But when Conrad introduced us that morning — something I thought he would've done long before today, like at the party he'd invited me to — she'd held out her limp hand for me to shake, and though her words were kind, the glimmer in her blue eyes was not. Surely she didn't see me as some sort of threat, did she? Conrad was old enough to be my father.

Having done the math, after pulling up more information on Conrad last night when I sat at home alone, I knew that Conrad had married his first wife when he was twenty-three, divorced four years later. During that time, he had obviously been with Sebastian's mother, because that was when she'd gotten pregnant. He'd then married his second wife when he was twenty-eight, divorced her when he was thirty. He was fifty-one now, and Aaliyah was twenty-one, which meant … Conrad had gotten Lauren pregnant when he had still been married to his second wife.

"Does she get along with Sebastian?" I inquired, fearing I might've overstepped with that question, but I wanted to know. I wanted to know what would've possessed Conrad to abandon his child. Married or not, he should have taken responsibility for his actions.

"Sebastian doesn't really get along with anyone," Aaliyah said with a traffic-stopping grin. "Except for me."

I was happy to hear that their relationship was good. Sebastian needed someone in his corner, and unfortunately, it didn't look like he had his father backing him up.

"I thought he'd be going to Vegas," I said softly.

Aaliyah looked at me and her smile fell. "He was supposed to. I don't know what happened, but it sounds like my father told him to stay home."

My eyebrows shot into my hairline. Was she serious? Why would he do that? "Was it before or after he asked me to come along?"

The question was out before I could stop myself. I watched Aaliyah, waiting for her to brush me off or scold me for being too nosey. She didn't. She only sighed and said, "I honestly don't know. I was just as surprised as you to find out he wasn't going. I was looking forward to it."

"Have you been to Vegas before?"

"Yes. But not since I turned twenty-one. Sebastian promised to take me out to celebrate when we got there. That was his birthday present to me."

My stomach plummeted to my feet. Sebastian had promised to take his sister to Vegas, and yet he wasn't there with her. That didn't sit well with me. Sebastian didn't seem like the kind of guy who would let his sister down. He'd been let down so many times in his life, I just couldn't picture him doing that to someone.

The attendant delivered breakfast to us on trays, and our conversation dwindled down to mere pleasantries. If I had to guess, Aaliyah was thinking about the fact that her brother wasn't there with us. Truth was, I was thinking about it, too.

I missed him.

Although we'd only been together a short time, every minute we were apart felt like an eternity. In such a short time, we had established a connection, something stronger than even I had anticipated. Having spent the night with him, his arms wrapped around me, his body heat warming me … being without him was almost painful.

I knew I probably shouldn't be getting too attached to him. As much as I wanted to believe in happy ever after, I had to wonder whether there were alternate forces working against Sebastian and me. After all, I did work for his father — a man who had kept Sebastian a secret for all these years. I could understand Conrad being concerned about what people would say. He had impregnated an underage girl, and he'd been married at the time. But to think that his reputation could have caused him to abandon his own child… That made me want to throw something at him.

After I had picked at my food for a few minutes, I gave up. I wasn't hungry. My nerves were shot to hell, and I knew I had to spend the next four days with Conrad and his family. Well, *part* of his family. Working would likely be the only thing that could keep my mind occupied, and even then, I feared I wasn't going to be able to stop thinking about Sebastian.

I wasn't sure I would ever stop thinking about him. No matter what was going on.

Chapter Twelve

Sebastian

Tuesday
In Vegas

My plane landed ten minutes earlier than anticipated, which meant I had to wait a little longer than I wanted to, but I was okay with that. Really. It beat the alternative of being late, which would have been just my luck.

Early was good.

Well, I was trying to be okay with being ahead of schedule, but Leif wouldn't shut the hell up, and he was irritating the shit out of me with his incessant rambling. He was raring to go, ready to toss quarters into the slot machines that lined the center aisles through the terminal. I had already told him to go for it, but then he got distracted when we passed a Cinnabon. Apparently, he was hungry.

I was hungry. But not for food.

Leaving Leif in line at the restaurant, I checked the monitors to confirm the gate I was supposed to be going to. Seeing that the plane was on time, I made my way past the many shops and restaurants, dodging passengers who seemed to be in a hurry.

When I reached my destination, I glanced around, noticing that the travelers waiting for the next flight were all sitting, which meant the plane that had arrived hadn't released the passengers yet. As I propped myself against the wall, I stared out the huge panes of glass, willing the people to get off the damn plane that sat just outside the window. It had only been sitting at the gate for a minute, maybe two, and I was ready to storm the damn thing.

But I didn't. Probably not a wise idea in an airport.

So, I stood there, leaning against a pillar while I waited, pretending to be casual. I wasn't even worried whether or not someone snagged my luggage, which was probably spinning around a carousel all alone at this point, because the only place I wanted to be was right there.

I glanced over my shoulder to see if Leif had returned, and when I turned back, there she was.

My heart stuttered in my chest.

I get it, I was acting like a fucking pansy, but shit, I couldn't help it. When it came to Payton, I found myself feeling and doing a lot of crazy shit. She was, by far, the most beautiful woman in the entire world with her long dark hair, her big hazel eyes, flawless skin, and her kissable lips.

And just like the first time I'd seen her, my heart skipped a beat and my hands began to sweat.

Payton was smiling and offering a thank-you to the airline personnel who stood near the door she was currently walking through. I don't think she noticed me, and that was all right. I just wanted to look at her for another minute without interruption. I'd done it the other night when she'd spent the night. Lying in my bed with Payton my arms, I had watched her sleep until I couldn't take it anymore. Not wanting to wake her, I had snuck down to the workout room. What had happened when she'd joined me had been unexpected but something I would never forget.

And now, here she was.

"Payton." I watched her look around, and the instant our eyes met, the smile she bestowed me with had my heart thudding painfully in my chest, the air rushing from my lungs.

"Sebastian." My name was but a whisper on her lips, but I heard it as though someone had shoved a fucking megaphone in my ear. I smiled, watching her eyes light up in surprise.

Before I could move, before I could reach for her, there was my father. His glare should have incinerated me right there on the spot. I watched him look around briefly before he started my way. Rather than deal with him, I took matters into my own hands. Someone needed to remind him that I was twenty-five years old and I made my own damn decisions. If he didn't want me there, fine. That didn't mean I wasn't going to show up anyway.

But I had wanted to surprise Payton, and based on the way she was watching me, I was pretty sure I'd succeeded.

"Why the fuck are—" Conrad's question was cut off when my sister ran over to me, throwing her arms around my neck. I merely smirked back at Conrad over Aaliyah's shoulder. His frown deepened.

"Sebastian! You made it!" Aaliyah squealed loud enough to rouse the dead, but then her voice lowered and she added, "Thank God."

I smiled, my eyes still locked with Conrad's.

When Aaliyah released me, I moved to Payton, taking her carry-on bag from her shoulder and hefting it onto mine before taking her hand and pulling her to me. I planted a quick kiss to her lips and then took a step back and watched her.

Her eyes were wide, her mouth hanging open just slightly, and she looked so damn cute I wanted to pick her up and carry her off into the sunset like some sort of knight in shining fucking armor. Like I said, crazy shit was going through my head these days.

I ignored my thoughts, figuring it would be a little too uncivilized.

"You ready?" I asked Payton, ignoring the glare from my father.

"Where do you think you're going?" Conrad asked, his voice much lower than before.

"I'll make sure she's at work when she needs to be there," I promised him. "Don't worry about her. She's safe with me."

The look I shot him dared him to argue with me. I was tired of his petty bullshit. Like I had vowed the other night, no one was going to keep her from me. Certainly not Conrad.

"Payton," Conrad called, and I watched as she turned to him.

"Daddy," Aaliyah interrupted, coming to stand in front of Conrad, her slender fingers resting gently on his arm. "Don't do this, please."

"Aaliyah, stay out of this," Lauren insisted, her tone as icy as her gaze.

My sister took instruction about as well as I did. "Mother..."

"You stay with her, Aaliyah," Conrad interrupted before Aaliyah could finish her sentence.

"Of course," Aaliyah said in that sweet voice that she used when she told them what they wanted to hear. "She has your itinerary. We'll make sure she gets where she needs to be."

That was my sister for you.

"Not 'we,' Aaliyah," Conrad scolded, his gaze flipping to me before returning to her. "You."

"Yes, Daddy."

With my arm around Payton, I turned, smirking at my father as I did. As I'd said before, I lived to piss off the old man. But honestly, this wasn't about him. The only reason I'd come to Vegas after he'd informed me that I wasn't needed or wanted was so that I could be with Payton. Five days away from her was just a little more than I could bear, and I wasn't going to risk the chaos returning, especially not when she'd managed to calm me so thoroughly.

Leif joined us just as I was leading Payton away from Conrad. His smile widened when he turned his attention to Aaliyah, reaching for her bag and hefting it onto his brawny shoulder. I wanted to slap the smirk off his face. I knew the main reason he had come with me was so that he could spend some time with my sister. The guy was infatuated with her. As much as I wanted to stand between them, I knew that it wasn't my place to make decisions for her. And since I was dealing with that firsthand thanks to Conrad's interference, I decided that during my time in Vegas, I was going to let them figure it out for themselves.

Then, when we were back home, I'd pound him into the ground if he hurt her.

"I can't believe you came," Payton whispered, looking up at me as we maneuvered through the hordes of passengers coming and going in the terminal.

I leaned over and kissed the top of her head as we walked. "Angel, nothing would've kept me away from you. Nothing."

Chapter Thirteen

Sebastian

Forty-five minutes later, the four of us were walking into Aria. I had surprised Aaliyah with a hotel change, but my sister didn't seem to mind at all. Considering my father was staying at Caesar's Palace, the hotel we'd all previously been booked at, I wasn't about to stay there even though I could have snagged a villa that would've blown Payton's mind.

But this was right up our alley, a hotel that catered more to our age anyway. And we wouldn't run the risk of encountering Conrad or Lauren.

Once we were inside, we made our way to the check-in desk. Leif raided the food area while I stepped up to the counter, encountering the woman who would be helping me. She didn't look at all happy to see me, and her eyes immediately went to my lip ring, then to my eyebrow. Never once did she meet my gaze.

Aaliyah apparently found the process amusing and insisted that Payton remain there to watch.

This happened to me a lot. And, just as Aaliyah did, I often found it comical. Today I was a little antsy, not wanting to spend time fucking with the red-tape bullshit, preferring instead to be with Payton. But this was one of those things that had to be done. Therefore, I might as well enjoy myself.

Apparently, in order to be significantly wealthy, you must have a certain look about you. Or so it seemed based on the reaction I frequently received. In my opinion, I looked rather normal. Aside from the piercings and the tattoos, there wasn't anything about me that stood out. I didn't have an entourage; therefore, they didn't figure me to be a celebrity — which I certainly was not.

"Mister…" The lady glanced at the computer screen and then back to me.

"Trovato," I said, tolerating her rudeness for the moment.

"Could you spell that?"

Okay, so she was clearly going to push me to my limits, but I indulged her and spelled out my name. Very, very slowly. That earned me a sneer.

"Yes." She glanced down her nose at me and then back to the screen. "I show you've booked one of the sky villas."

I nodded.

She glanced over at Payton and Aaliyah before looking back at me. She leaned closer and lowered her voice, "Are you aware how much the room is going to be?"

"Hmmm," I pretended to ponder the question, leaning in and lowering my voice. "Did I *ask* how much it was going to be?"

"N-No, s-sir," the young woman stuttered, pulling back as though I'd slapped her. I had never in my life hit a woman, nor would I, but I could honestly say that had she been a man, she'd have been on the ground at that point.

"Then I'm not sure why you brought it up," I added a little less harshly, keeping my eyes trained on her.

The woman adjusted her clothing and then took a deep breath. "Then I'll just need your license and credit card."

Snatching my wallet from my back pocket, I flipped it open and pulled out my license and the lone credit card I kept on me at all times. I dropped them onto the counter and leisurely slid them toward her, never breaking eye contact.

As with most places I went, it wasn't until I dropped the infamous black card that I usually got eyed speculatively. The woman didn't disappoint.

That didn't stop her from comparing the license to the card, glancing at me and then to the picture on the card and back several times.

I, personally, found it entertaining.

So did Aaliyah.

Tired of playing the game because it left Payton standing there waiting, I leaned in and said, "Would you like me to get my personal banker on the phone? His name's Greg. I'll be happy to let you talk to him."

"No, sir," she said urgently, typing the information into the computer.

From that point on, the less-than-pleasant woman checked us in, and there was already someone waiting with our bags by the time I was handed the key cards. A few minutes later, we were stepping into the luxurious sky villa. The gentleman who brought our bags took them to the respective rooms where I instructed, and then, while I paid the tip, Aaliyah began dragging Payton around.

Leif, of course, was trying to play it cool. As cool as he was capable of anyway.

"You're a fancy bastard, you know that, man?" Leif stated when he came out of the guest room on the first floor. I had purposely put him there since there were two bedrooms upstairs. It was going to be my last-ditch effort to keep him as far from my sister as possible, and I could only hope that it worked.

"Shut the fuck up," I said as I made my way to the windows that overlooked the strip.

Although the hotel didn't sit directly on Las Vegas Blvd, we still had an awesome view and the best part, Conrad had no idea what hotel we were in.

Closing my eyes, I vowed that I wouldn't think about him for the rest of the trip. At least not more than I had to. As Aaliyah had told him, we would ensure that Payton got to where she needed to be when she needed to be there, but what I hadn't bothered to tell him was that I wasn't going to be far. He seemed to forget that as far as the show went, I fully intended to make an appearance as I did every year. After all, I knew a hell of a lot more than he did. I was just waiting for him to realize it.

I was probably going to be waiting a long damn time.

"So what're we gonna do first?" Aaliyah asked when she came traipsing down the stairs with Payton in tow.

"First, we need to figure out Payton's schedule," I informed them. I was going to keep my promise, but only because of Payton.

Snagging her purse from the table, Payton took it over to the leather couch and plopped down, pulling a stack of folded papers out and causing the rest of us to laugh. She looked up, wide-eyed. "What are y'all laughing at?"

"They make these things called smart phones," Leif informed her, trying to keep a straight face. "They've got all sorts of things on it, including a calendar. You don't have to kill a forest anymore."

Payton blushed, flattening the papers out on her lap and looking away.

When I passed Leif, I punched him in the arm. Hard. Unable to resist, I went to her, dropping just as dramatically onto the couch as she had, and pulled her against me, inhaling her sweet, sexy scent. From the moment I'd seen her in the airport, I'd wanted to strip her naked and bury myself inside her. But I'd refrained and knew I would probably have to a little longer, so touching her would have to be enough.

"Do you want me to beat his ass for talking shit?" I asked, also trying to keep from laughing.

Payton looked up at Leif, then over to me. She was clearly better at acting because she appeared to be considering my offer. "Let me think about that for a while," she said with a wry grin, her gaze darting back to Leif.

Smart guy, he took one step back and thrust his hands into his pockets.

"So, what's the plan?" I asked.

I'd been to enough of these trade shows to know when my father would be needed. Trovato, Inc. had representatives at the show who would manage everything when it came to the booth. Conrad likely wouldn't attend unless he was on a panel or conducting a seminar. And even those would be few and far between. But I knew he would be there sometime, which meant he would want Payton there.

Now, we just needed to get that out of the way so we could have a little fun.

Chapter Fourteen

Payton

Tuesday

After SEMA show

If I'd had any doubts before that Mr. Trovato was out to punish Sebastian, my mind was indeed set straight now. In turn, it also appeared that he was using me in order to accomplish his goal.

So far, the SEMA show wasn't all that bad. Rather interesting, actually. Between the cars, the exhibits, the people, and the excitement, it had been hard to remember that I was working. Especially when Sebastian was remaining close to my side. But Conrad had been dead set on ensuring I knew exactly why I was there. He had been disturbingly anal with his requests, and I had spent most of my time fetching things for him. At one point, he'd even sent me back to his hotel room in order to get a particular pen that he wanted to use. A pen. Like a writing utensil. Yes, that was what I considered disturbingly anal.

Something wasn't right, but it wasn't like I could say anything. After all, I was his assistant, and he was paying me to assist.

So, I'd spent the last few hours on my feet, following him around. If I wasn't getting him coffee, I was going in search of a specific booth to find a specific person so that I could set up a lunch or dinner while Mr. Trovato was there. Then I was on the phone, trying to make reservations or I was getting him water, or a particular pen that he didn't even bother to use.

What Conrad didn't realize was that I didn't mind. Not one bit. But only because Sebastian had insisted on being there with me. The entire time. So when I got Mr. Trovato coffee, Sebastian got me coffee. When I went in search of a person, I got to watch as people recognized and conversed with Sebastian as though he were some sort of mechanical super genius.

It was one of the most interesting days of my life, and it was now only six o'clock.

Sebastian and I had returned to the hotel alone. Leif was somewhere downstairs at the casino, and Aaliyah had spent the afternoon with her mother at a spa. We were all supposed to meet back at the hotel room by seven so we could go to dinner and then spend some time in the casino.

"Do I have time to shower?" I asked Sebastian when we made our way up the stairs to the bedroom he had claimed for us.

"Depends," he said, moving up behind me and sweeping my hair over my shoulder. The feel of his lips on my neck made my knees weak and my heart race. He must have realized the effect he had on me, because he wrapped his arms around my waist and pulled me into him. I could feel the evidence of his arousal against my lower back, and I was tempted to say to hell with dinner.

"On?" I asked, breathless, as he continued to brush his mouth over the sensitive skin of my neck.

"If you want me to join you or not."

The idea of getting in that huge glass shower with Sebastian was almost too good to pass up. But I knew that Leif and Aaliyah would be back soon, and if we had any intention of getting food and enjoying a little of the Vegas nightlife, we would have to avoid getting naked together.

"Okay, how about this," I said as I turned around to face him, sliding my hands up the hard planes of his chest and then wrapping my arms around his neck. "What if I change, and later, when we get back, we can spend some time in the giant tub. Alone."

Sebastian walked me backward until my back was against the wall and his muscular thigh pressed between my legs. Yeah, he was purposely making me crazy.

"I think that sounds like a plan," he whispered before crushing his mouth to mine, tangling his hand in my hair. Delicious bolts of pleasure darted from my scalp down to my core when he pulled my head back.

Yeah, if he kept doing that, dinner was going to be the last thing on my mind.

***

"So he really didn't tell you who he was when you came to the house?" Aaliyah asked, her smile wide, showing her perfectly straight, white teeth.

"He said he was a mechanic," I explained, pushing my plate away and reaching for my water.

Leif chuckled, staring back and forth between Sebastian and me.

"In my defense," Sebastian began, squeezing my knee beneath the table, "she assumed I was a mechanic."

"He made me believe no one was home to get the phone," I retorted quickly, grinning. In retrospect, it was a rather amusing story. And I liked the fact that it gave us an interesting first-time introduction story.

"So that's why you were all gaga over her at the party," Aaliyah said, her eyes glittering brightly as she laughed.

"Sebastian? Gaga? Damn I wish I had been there to see that," Leif added.

"If I recall correctly, you" — Sebastian pointed at Aaliyah — "went on and on about how cute Payton and Aaron were together."

Aaliyah's laugh had heads turning. "That's right. I remember that, too."

I smiled, remembering that Aaron had explicitly introduced himself to Aaliyah as my gay best friend who had been coerced into attending.

"And then you just happened to show up at the same restaurant?" Aaliyah asked, sipping her wine, clearly amused by the entire situation.

"Sports bar," Sebastian corrected, leaning back in his chair and reaching for my hand beneath the table, linking his fingers with mine.

The fact that he insisted on always touching me did strange things to my insides. If he wasn't holding my hand, he was touching my lower back or wrapping his arm around my shoulder. I found that I craved the feel of his rough skin against mine.

"Very interesting," Aaliyah said, placing her glass back on the table.

The waiter returned to place the check on the table, but Sebastian merely handed him his credit card without looking at the bill, and the guy sauntered off quickly.

"How's school going?" Leif asked Aaliyah, his expression changing from fun to serious all of a sudden.

I would admit that I didn't know Leif all that well, but even I could see the intense interest he had in Sebastian's sister. It was fascinating. The usual laid-back guy was replaced with someone who looked … nervous.

Leif was a good-looking guy with his messy dark hair and dark eyes. He was probably the same height as Sebastian, but he was bigger, bulkier compared to Sebastian's lean frame. Leif's hair was a bit too long, but he often hid it beneath a ball cap. Not tonight, though. Tonight he looked nice, wearing a pair of jeans and a button-up shirt, similar to what Sebastian was wearing.

"Boring," Aaliyah answered Leif, her blue eyes locking with Leif's brown eyes.

Oh, yeah, there was some powerful chemistry there. On both parts.

I cast a glance at Sebastian. He was pretending not to see the interest between his sister and his best friend. I squeezed his thigh, offering a little support. He didn't appear to be interfering, and after having to deal with Conrad all day, I was happy to see that. It was a pain in the ass to deal with someone who wanted to interfere. Sebastian, as amazing as I thought he was, wouldn't be any different if he thought he could be the one to keep those two apart.

"What are you majoring in?" I asked Aaliyah, trying to spur the conversation.

"Pharmaceutical science," Aaliyah said easily.

"Wow," I said, breathing out quickly. "That's great."

"It comes naturally for me," Aaliyah added, her gaze drifting back to Leif.

"What do you do?" I asked Leif when no one else said anything.

"I'm a shop foreman," he informed me.

"What type of shop?"

"Body shop."

"Small world. My dad owns a body shop."

"Yeah? In Austin?"

"Yes. Been in business now for twenty-eight years."

"Times are tough," Leif said, his full attention sliding my way. "With the big companies invading Austin's market, we're losing traction fast. Half the time I get up in the morning not knowing whether or not I'll have a job by the end of the day."

I knew just what he was talking about because I'd heard my parents arguing about it. Some of the larger conglomerates were coming into Austin and buying up all of the mom-and-pop shops, taking them over and cutting jobs. Since my mother had mentioned that the shop wasn't doing great financially, I knew my father was dealing with the same issues Leif was. I hadn't thought much of it, but I made a mental note to check in with my parents when I got back to Austin. At least then maybe they wouldn't be so worried that I'd gone off to Las Vegas without much notice.

"How's your mom?" Aaliyah asked Leif.

"Good. She's … uh…" Leif glanced at Sebastian and then back to Aaliyah. "She's moving in with her boyfriend. Well, technically, I guess he's moving in with her."

"The cop?" Aaliyah asked.

"Detective. Yeah."

"It's about time," Aaliyah said, reaching for her wineglass again.

Leif chuckled. "I guess so. They've been dating for a couple of years," he explained, looking at me again. "His name's Tom. Nice guy. My mother finally agreed to marry him."

"That's great," I said, hoping that was really the case.

I was a little distracted by the way Aaliyah was hanging on to Leif's every word. She clearly knew a lot about him, which meant that either she and Leif talked or she and Sebastian did. From what I could tell, Aaliyah was fond of her brother, but I didn't get the vibe that they talked a lot. Why that was, I didn't know.

"Which is why Leif's moving into my place for a while. He's been staying with his mother so she didn't have to be alone. Now that she won't be, she's kicking him to the curb," Sebastian said, grinning.

"She is not." Leif laughed. "I'm twenty-five years old. I think it's time I moved out anyway."

I watched Aaliyah's reaction to that news, and I saw the gleam in her bright blue eyes. I think she liked the idea of Leif moving closer to where she was. Now, whether or not Conrad and her mother would approve, that would probably be an entirely different story.

"Hey, you still plannin' to do the race on Saturday?" Leif asked Sebastian directly, completely changing the subject.

My head snapped toward him, my eyes studying his face. A race.

He gently squeezed my hand beneath the table as he answered Leif with an affirmative nod. "I said I'd be there."

There was a hint of anger in his tone, and I noticed the storm clouds brewing in his brilliant gold gaze. I didn't know whether or not there was a story there, but when Leif didn't push the issue, I decided not to as well. I'd talk to Sebastian about it later.

The waiter returned with the leather folder containing the bill, and Sebastian quickly scribbled his name and retrieved his credit card.

"So, what's the plan for tonight?" Aaliyah asked, finishing off her wine.

"I say we head out to the casino, drop some money in the machine, and see if we can get lucky," Leif replied.

"I'm already lucky," Sebastian mumbled, his hand squeezing mine again beneath the table.

The man had the ability to make me swoon. I wasn't sure how someone could be so sweet and so intense at the same time, but Sebastian walked a very fine line. He treated me like I was a princess, all while he seemed to be battling the storm clouds that continued to brew in his gaze.

"Then what are we waiting for?" Leif asked, pushing his chair back and then standing behind Aaliyah, helping her to her feet.

Sebastian did the same for me and I blushed. I wasn't used to this sort of treatment.

As we started to walk out of the restaurant, Sebastian leaned over and whispered against my ear, "Just note that when we're done, I'm going to spend the rest of the night buried so deep inside you that you forget your own name."

And just like that, my body ignited into a fireball. I was surprised I managed to keep upright after that erotic promise.

"All right. On to the casino," Leif announced.

Casino?

What casino?

Chapter Fifteen

Sebastian

It was a good thing that my addictive personality didn't spill over into everything I did. For the last two hours, I'd remained at Payton's side, sitting at a slot machine and watching as she hit buttons and racked up the dollars. First timer's luck, I guess. But whatever it was, the woman looked good doing it.

Leif and Aaliyah had disappeared soon after dinner — together — and I forced them to the back of my mind. Leif was a good guy. He might be a man whore, but he was always safe, and I knew he would treat my sister with respect. He knew if he didn't, I'd beat his ass to a pulp, but that was beside the point.

Payton yawned and I grinned, glancing down at my watch. "It's three o'clock. What do you say we head up to the room?"

"Three o'clock? In the morning?" she asked, her eyes wide.

"Yep."

"But all these people are still out." She gestured toward the people milling about inside the casino, most of them playing table games not too far away from where we sat.

"Sin City never sleeps," I told her, turning her in her chair to face me more fully.

"Conrad's gonna kill me tomorrow."

"Technically that's today, and I'd prefer we don't talk about him."

"Sorry," she said with a sweet grin. When she leaned forward, pressing her lips to mine, I had to refrain from pulling her onto my lap. I'd been sporting an aching hard-on for the last few hours, and whenever she touched me, I had to fight back the urge to sneak her into a dark corner and devour her whole.

Considering this was Vegas and every corner, dark or otherwise, had a camera, I didn't think that was a wise idea. After all, we had a great room upstairs just waiting for us.

"I'm ready when you are," she finally said.

I hit the *change* button on the machine and grabbed the ticket when it printed. We made our way to a machine that cashed out the tickets, and I handed her the money that it spit out.

"That's *your* money," she said, refusing to take it, her hands wrapped tightly around my bicep.

I snagged a twenty-dollar bill from the pile, which was what she'd started with, and held the remaining out for her to take. "This is mine," I said, holding up the bill between two fingers. "The rest is yours. You won it fair and square."

Payton's eyes narrowed as she stared down at the money in my hand. She'd done well, raking in roughly five hundred in just a few hours. Granted, this was Vegas and you could easily lose twice that much in half the time, so it wasn't something I usually did when I visited.

Reaching for Payton's hand, I twined my fingers with hers and led her to the elevator that would take us to our room.

As soon as we were in the room, I listened to make sure that no one else had come back already. When I was met with silence, I shut the door and pulled Payton to me. "How about that bath?"

"Sounds like heaven."

More so than she knew.

Surprising her, I slid my hands down her ass, gripping her thighs and lifting her, forcing her to wrap her legs around my waist. With my arms bracing her, I headed for the stairs that would take us to our second-floor bedroom.

"You're gonna hurt your back." She giggled, her arms wrapped tightly around my neck.

"I'm young, I'll deal."

Once we were in our room, I closed and locked the door before sliding her down my body until her feet touched the floor. The sexy black dress she'd put on was what I attacked first, trying to rein in my hunger for her as I lowered the zipper and allowed the strapless number to slide to the floor.

"Have I mentioned how much I love that dress?" I asked.

"You might've said something a time or two," she whispered softly, smiling over her shoulder at me.

"You look incredible in it. But you look even better out of it."

In the soft light of the bedroom, I could see the pink that infused her cheeks. Again, I felt invincible. Payton's reactions were so damn sweet, so innocent. She wasn't like other women I'd been with, always trying to prove how hot she was. No, Payton was the opposite, and truth be told, she was far sexier than any woman I'd ever met.

It was difficult not to pick her up and toss her on the bed as she stood before me in a pair of red satin panties and a matching strapless bra. When she moved closer, I was forced to lift my gaze in order to look at her face, letting my eyes graze her mouth briefly.

She made quick work of unhooking the buttons on my shirt. I helped her by releasing the cuffs and then letting the white cotton slide down my arms and fall to the floor. I wanted her hands on my bare skin, and I wasn't disappointed. Her soft, cool fingers slid over my chest and then up to cup my face.

"I'm so glad you're here," she whispered, her expression serious. "I thought I was going to have to spend five days away from you."

"I wasn't going to miss it," I told her.

I didn't want to tell her that being away from her for the last two nights had been difficult enough. I didn't want to push her too hard, but I wasn't sure how long I would be able to go without letting her know how I felt about her. I'd never felt this way about a woman, never wanted a woman to stay the night and certainly never for more than one night. Lust was a far cry from what I felt for Payton, and before her, that was the extent of any emotion that a woman had stirred in me.

But with Payton, I felt an overwhelming need to keep her close, listen to her laugh, make her smile, and make sure that no one hurt her. Spending even a few minutes apart was excruciating and not just because the chaos returned with a vengeance when she wasn't with me. The truth was, I loved her. I had fallen hard and fast, and the descent hadn't stopped yet. I was still falling for her, every second of every day.

"Come on," I said, leaning down and pressing my lips to hers. "Let's get naked and wet."

Payton giggled and her cheeks turned a brighter shade of red, which I found extremely sexy.

A few minutes later, we were in the bathtub, the only light coming from the lamp in the bedroom and the glow of the buildings outside the floor-to-ceiling windows.

"This is…" Payton's words trailed off as I slid my hands down her chest, cupping her breasts and kneading them gently while I pressed my lips to her ear.

"It's what?" I breathed against her neck.

"Beautiful," she said, her tone raspy and so damn sexy my cock throbbed with anticipation.

Neither of us said anything for long minutes while I continued to caress her slowly, sliding my hands down her stomach, teasing her beneath the water briefly before returning my hands to her breasts. When I tweaked her nipples gently, her breath hitched.

"You like that?" I asked, my throat dry.

"Yes," she moaned, pushing back against me while thrusting her breasts into my hands.

I pinched her nipples more firmly, teasing her more insistently.

"Sebastian."

The way she said my name sent chills down my spine. "Say my name again," I instructed.

"Sebastian." Her voice lowered, her hands gripping my thighs more firmly as she began to squirm against my hands. "I need more."

Sliding one hand down beneath the water again, I teased her clit, stroking softly. I didn't want to rush, although my dick had other ideas. But I wasn't going to waste this moment. I continued to tease her, slipping my finger inside her until she was moaning loudly, my name on her lips like a beacon calling me home.

"Oh, God, Sebastian … I'm gonna…"

"Come for me, Angel," I whispered against her ear, thrusting my finger inside her while I pinched her nipple between my thumb and forefinger.

Her strangled cry, along with her short nails digging into my thighs, had my body throbbing. The way her body gripped my finger, her climax tightening every muscle, I was surprised I didn't detonate right then and there.

When she came down from her release, I allowed the silence to surround us while we sat there in the warm water, her body relaxing into mine. I continued to slide my hands up and down her smooth, wet skin while we stared out into the night sky, the lights of the Vegas strip providing an incredible backdrop for what was turning out to be the most incredible evening.

When the water began to cool, I helped her out of the tub, wrapped a towel around her, and then dried myself off quickly. Dropping my towel to the floor, I swept Payton off her feet, carrying her to the bed and lowering her gently.

My intentions had been good. I was going to go slow, savor her for hours, but the next thing I knew, Payton was pulling me on top of her. One of her arms snaked around my neck, her mouth meeting mine while her other hand slid between our bodies. She found my erection hard and rigid between us, and her soft fingers wrapping around me had me trying to catch my breath.

When she aligned our bodies, guiding me inside her, I pulled my lips from hers and stared into her eyes as I sank into her. As I slid deeper, her eyes closed, her breaths becoming labored as she pressed her hips up to meet mine.

"Open your eyes," I instructed. "Look at me, Angel."

Payton's eyes slowly slid open, our gazes meeting, holding as I pumped my hips gently, burying myself deep and then retreating slowly.

"I could do this forever, you know," I said with a wry grin.

"Me, too." She was breathless, her fingernails digging into my back.

I needed her. More than I needed anything else. More than oxygen and water, more than racing, more than…

"Sebastian," she said, her eyes still locked with mine.

"Oh, God, you feel so damn good," I growled, thrusting into her more forcefully, pushing us both closer and closer to the edge. "Payton."

The noise in my head that I'd dealt with for so long was quieter than it had ever been, and I knew without a doubt that she was the reason. She was meant for me, the only thing in the world that could possibly keep me from shattering into a million pieces. And here she was, her lips seeking mine as I drove into her deeper, harder, faster. Her legs wrapped around my hips, pulling me to her, and I couldn't hold back. Our sweat-slick bodies slid together, our breaths mingling as I continued to drive into her, burying myself as deep as possible, just as I'd promised. I wanted her to think of me and only me.

"Payton," I breathed against her mouth. "Angel, you fucking unhinge me. Come for me, baby. Come *with* me."

She cried out, but I captured the sound with my mouth as we both flew over the edge, my body consumed by her. I didn't want to let her go. Not now, not ever. My release seemed to go on forever, and as I fought for air, I pulled back and stared down into her beautiful face, the next words out of my mouth surprising us both. "You own me." I took a deep breath and added, "I love you."

Chapter Sixteen

Payton

My heart skipped a beat.

Maybe two.

Hell, it might've stopped beating altogether when Sebastian whispered those three words. The three words I had never heard from a man's mouth. Not like this.

My heart expanded in my chest, and a smile quickly followed. "I love you," I whispered back, the words coming so naturally. I didn't have to think about it. I'd already known that I had fallen for Sebastian, far sooner than I ever thought I would.

Sebastian cupped my face with his hand as he watched me. I couldn't tell what he was thinking, but for the first time, there weren't any storm clouds gathered in his beautiful gaze. He seemed to be at peace, and I didn't know if that was because of what I'd said or just the overwhelming feelings that seemed to be coursing between us.

"Hold that thought," he whispered, smiling before he slipped out of the bed and padded naked to the bathroom. I stared after him, peeking at his incredibly fine back side, admiring the angel wings across his back.

Ironic how he called me angel, yet he seemed to have been sent here for me. I still had a hard time wrapping my mind around all that had happened in the last couple of weeks. Between the dreams that had started, all starring a man I would soon meet, and then to stumble upon him at my boss's house, my dreams literally coming to life… Sometimes I wondered if it was too good to be true.

Sebastian returned, a washcloth in his hand. My body was so sated I could hardly move. And when he used the warm cloth to clean between my sore thighs, I fought the blush that crept up my neck. He disappeared once more and returned a minute later, sliding into bed beside me, pulling the covers up over us both before spooning behind me.

Neither of us said anything for long minutes, the only sound coming from the ceiling fan spinning up high on the ceiling.

"Is there meaning behind the angel wings?" I asked, placing my arm over his where he was wrapped around me.

"Yeah," he whispered softly, his breath blowing my hair.

I giggled. "Are you going to tell me what it is?"

"If you ask nicely," he replied, his arms tightening around me.

"Please?"

"I got the wings as a way to keep myself aware of which direction I needed to go. Without my mother here…"

I squeezed his hand. "Tell me."

"When my mother died, I had no one. One day she was there, then she was gone. My best friend in the entire world stolen from me. From the minute the police showed up at the apartment, my life changed in every way that mattered.

"After making sure that I knew there were no other options, that he wasn't choosing me but rather was being saddled with me, Conrad took me in. He didn't treat me like his son. Hell, I was lucky that he at least treated me like the hired help. And my new instant family couldn't have cared less who I was or why I was there. I remember Aaliyah back then. She wasn't nice to me at first, but I couldn't blame her. It took a few years before she finally came to accept me.

"I started acting out immediately, fighting with anyone and everyone. I stopped trying in school, came home whenever I wanted. I don't think anyone really noticed. I had no one to make sure I was doing what I should, no one to tell me that they loved me or that they'd miss me when I was gone." Sebastian paused. I heard him swallow hard before continuing. "When I turned eighteen, I went straight to the tattoo shop, gave them my design. I remember the guy thought it was cool but wanted to enhance it. I didn't let him modify it because the design had come to me in a dream. A dream I had of my mother.

"She came back. Just the one time. She came back, and she told me that I needed to pull it together. I was making a mess of my life before I even knew the impact it would have. I had contemplated dropping out of high school at sixteen because it just didn't matter. But in that dream, my mother told me that I was making a mistake. It was then that I decided I needed something to keep me moving in the right direction. Something to remind me of the path I should be on, because no one was pointing me there. Sometimes the right path isn't as obvious as it should be, no matter who you are. It's even less apparent when you're fourteen years old and your best friend dies, the only person who ever told me they loved me."

I couldn't hold back the sob that ripped through my chest at Sebastian's words. Every word he spoke was laced with emotion, and I knew it was hard for him to talk about his mother, but I wanted to hear. I wanted to know him. To know everything about him. I was grateful when Sebastian held me tighter but continued to talk.

"Even though I may not see the wings, I know they're there. And when it seems that I'm going too far from where I should be, I think of her. She's behind me, pushing me forward. I know where she is, and I'm bound and determined that one day I *will* see her again." Sebastian's voice hitched and it broke my heart. I couldn't stop the tears from rolling down my cheeks and landing on the pillow.

The idea of Sebastian spending most of his life without someone to tell him that they loved him, without someone to show him each and every day just how important he was made the tears fall faster. I could hardly swallow past the lump in my throat.

"Don't cry for me, Payton," Sebastian whispered in my ear, pulling me against him.

I tried not to, but I couldn't stop myself. The sobs came harder, my body shuddering as I replayed his statement over and over in my head. Several minutes passed before I managed to collect myself enough to speak. I turned my head to try and look at him over my shoulder. "I love you, Sebastian." He pressed his lips to my cheek, kissing away one of my tears. "And I'm going to make sure I tell you so every single day."

We lay in silence for a while. I listened to him breathe, and I thought he had fallen asleep, so I was giving in to my exhaustion but trying to hang on for a few more minutes because I just wanted to be there with him.

Just as my eyes were drifting closed, Sebastian spoke. "You didn't seem surprised when I told you that Conrad was my father."

I forced them open, turning in his arms so that I could rest my head against his chest. I wanted to touch him, because when I did, there was a connection there that felt surreal. One that gave me the feeling — real or perceived, I wasn't sure — that nothing could go wrong in the world as long as he was with me.

"Too many coincidences," I told him softly. "You were at his house, then at the party. It just seemed logical to me."

"Logical," Sebastian huffed.

I tapped his chest lightly. "You know what I mean." I sighed, snuggling closer to him. The silence returned for several long seconds before I said, "Do you think this is happening too fast?"

I felt his body tense, his arm tightening around me. "No, I don't."

His tone was firm, leaving no room for argument, so I didn't say anything more. I let the silence drift over me, relishing the warmth of Sebastian's body against mine, the steady beat of his heart against my ear. As for my thoughts on whether or not we were moving too fast, I agreed with Sebastian. I didn't think it was too fast, either. In fact, when I was with him, time seemed to stand still; therefore, the actual measurement was nearly impossible.

I loved this man.

I don't know how much time passed, but I was slowly drifting off to sleep when I heard Sebastian whisper, "I love you, Angel. More than anyone. I swear I'll never let my demons come between us."

Chapter Seventeen

Payton
Wednesday

The following morning, I woke to the sound of music. A little disoriented, I forced my eyes open and looked around the room. The sun was shining through the floor-to-ceiling windows, warming my face. The music started again, and I realized it was my cell phone. I fumbled out of bed, gripping the sheet to my naked body, and found my purse on the floor by the door, where I'd left it when we'd come in last night. Or rather that morning.

What I thought was a phone call was actually the alarm that I'd set. I glanced at the clock on my phone, and panic set in. I was supposed to meet Conrad at his hotel that morning for a business breakfast — his words, not mine. He'd informed me of my required attendance the day before, just as I was leaving the show for the evening. I hadn't mentioned it to Sebastian, because Conrad had explicitly informed me that Sebastian was not invited and that if I valued my job, I wouldn't share that information with him.

And yes, that statement had struck me as odd, but Conrad was my boss, so I'd merely agreed with him. What else could I do?

"Shit," I grumbled, tossing the phone onto the bed and rushing into the bathroom.

It hadn't dawned on me until then that Sebastian wasn't anywhere in sight. I'd woken up alone, and he wasn't in the bathroom, either. Rather than try to find him and waste time I didn't have, I hopped in the shower and hurried through getting ready.

By the time I was dressed, my makeup done, and my hair dried, I still hadn't seen Sebastian, which worried me. I needed to be at the restaurant in less than twenty minutes, which meant I was going to have to figure out the best way to get there if no one was around to get me there. Damn it. I knew I should have thought this through all the way. Not telling Sebastian meant that I had to find my own transportation. Granted, I was an adult. I knew that I could hail a cab downstairs, but this was Las Vegas, and truth was, being alone out there just made me nervous.

Resigning myself to getting a cab at the main entrance to the casino, I grabbed my purse, dropped my cell phone inside, and then opened the bedroom door.

I was met with silence.

Crap.

From where I stood, I could see that Aaliyah's bedroom door was open and the bed wasn't made. I took the stairs as fast as I dared, proud of myself for not taking a header to the first floor. Once downstairs, I headed for the door, still not seeing a soul. I glanced back at the guest bedroom, and that door was open as well, the bed in there made.

Where the hell was everyone?

I didn't have time to waste trying to figure it out, though. I was going to be late, and Conrad was already in rare form — I didn't see any reason to piss him off more. I stopped at the check-in desk where we'd come in, and a nice woman there informed me that she would have a limo take me to Conrad's hotel. I double-timed it to the main doors and stepped outside to the sound of horns blaring and people talking.

"Ms. Fowler?" a gentleman standing beside a waiting limo called my name, and I hurried toward him, snagging a couple of dollars from my purse and shoving them toward him before darting inside the car.

Directions weren't necessary; apparently the desk lady had taken care of that for me. A few minutes later, after a hair-raising trip a few miles down the strip, the limo was pulling into Caesar's Palace. Once parked, the driver swiftly exited the vehicle to help me out. I handed him more money, offered a quick thank you, and then practically ran inside.

By the time I arrived at the restaurant I had agreed to meet Conrad and his wife at, I was sweating and out of breath. Who knew that power walking through a hotel would be the equivalent of running ten miles?

I gave my name to the hostess, and she promptly led me toward the back. I swallowed back my nerves as I approached the table, straightening my skirt and drying my now sweaty palms. Conrad and his wife had their backs to me, and on the opposite side was a young man I hadn't seen before. He certainly wasn't one of the people who Conrad had insisted I seek out and offer a dinner invitation to.

The guy looked up at me and smiled, causing Conrad to glance over his shoulder.

"There she is," Conrad greeted me kindly. Much kinder than I expected, considering I was at least ten minutes late.

"I'm so sorry I'm late," I said quickly, trying not to sound so out of breath.

"No need to apologize. I'd like you to meet Trevor. Trevor, this is my assistant, Payton Fowler. Payton, Trevor is Lauren's nephew."

"Nice to meet you, Payton."

I accepted Trevor's hand, shaking it gently. He was looking at me oddly, and I wondered whether or not I had something on my face. When he pulled out my chair, praying that I didn't have a stray streak of lip gloss, I subtly slid my hand over my mouth. I figured anything was possible given how rattled I was.

"Good morning, Payton," Lauren said icily, her blue gaze pinning me in place.

I had learned since meeting her the day before that she had two settings: lukewarm and icy. Neither of them made me feel comfortable. It looked as though she'd doubled up on the ice this morning. "Good morning," I replied, not wanting to be rude.

"We were just about to order," Conrad told me.

I felt incredibly awkward sitting at the table with them. First of all, it was strange to be having breakfast with my boss, who happened to also be my boyfriend's father. Secondly, the guy sitting next to me was much closer to my age than Conrad's, and I was curious as to why, exactly, he was there. Sure, being related to Lauren made sense, but not in regard to why I would have been invited to breakfast to meet him.

After perusing the menu for a moment, I made a selection, and after the waiter came and took our order, I sat patiently, trying to figure out just what I was supposed to be doing at this meeting.

"Conrad's told me so much about you," Trevor said, dragging my attention from rearranging my napkin on my lap. His voice was deep and smooth, his eyes the same icy blue as Lauren's. He seemed nice enough, clean cut, well dressed, but there was something that bothered me about him. Something I couldn't put my finger on.

I had no idea what to say to his comment, so I smiled.

"Trevor is in the process of moving to Austin," Conrad told me, and my eyes widened as I looked back at him.

"He's been having a little trouble," Lauren added, glancing over at Trevor, "but we've taken care of all that now. I think it'll be good for him to start over."

"Do you live here?" I asked Trevor, still trying to figure out why he was in Vegas.

"No. Conrad called me up and invited me. I'm considering a…" Trevor's eyes traveled over to Conrad and then back to me before he continued. "A career change."

When he didn't elaborate, I blurted out the first thing that came to mind. "What is it that you do?"

"I'm a mechanic."

Warning bells sounded in my head, and I wasn't sure why. Something wasn't right. Why would Lauren's nephew be having breakfast with us in Vegas if he didn't live there? More specifically, why was I having breakfast with them? Clearly, I was the odd man out. Hoping there was a logical reason, I waited patiently for someone to enlighten me.

I was obviously going to wait all day, because Lauren, Trevor, and Conrad began talking. They weren't talking business, which made me even more uncomfortable, but I tried my best to hide my distress.

My cell phone chimed from my purse, and I glanced around, wondering if it would be incredibly rude to answer while I was sitting at the table. After all, the three of them seemed to be ignoring me. Figuring it wouldn't help the situation, I kindly asked to be excused, pretending to need to go to the restroom. Instead, I slipped out of the restaurant and onto the casino floor, grabbing my phone out of my purse.

Where are you?

The text came from Sebastian.

Breakfast with your father.

What the fuck?

I hesitated before responding, but I was still creeped out by the whole thing, so I figured telling Sebastian couldn't hurt. At least then he'd know where I was if I needed him.

He insisted that I meet him and he told me not to tell you.

What restaurant?

I quickly typed the name of the restaurant and then informed Sebastian I would see him back at the hotel in an hour. When I didn't receive a response, I tossed my phone back in my purse and returned to the table. The food had been brought out, and the three occupants seemed to be waiting for me. I sighed before making my way over and sliding into my seat, pretending that I wasn't unnerved by the whole situation.

I didn't think I was doing a very good job. But I really didn't care.

Chapter Eighteen

Sebastian

I was on the verge of losing my damned mind.

Leif was just lucky that I was more concerned about Payton than the fact that he had dragged my sister to a strip club, gotten rip-roaring drunk, and then opted to spend the night in a casino in downtown Las Vegas versus coming back to the room. How the fuck they'd ended up downtown was beyond me, but the two of them weren't talking, so it wasn't likely that I was going to find out from either of them.

Whatever had happened between them had left them both pissed off at one another, refusing to talk. In fact, I had been forced out of bed at five-thirty because Aaliyah had refused to get into the car with Leif to come back to the hotel. I'd had to get a cab to take me to the Golden Nugget and wait while I went in and practically forced her out to the car.

At the last fucking minute, Leif had refused to go with us, and I'd been close to ripping his nose off his fucking face because I was so pissed. He was acting like a fucking child, and I didn't have time to play games with these idiots.

Then, to make matters worse, when I'd gotten back to the hotel, Payton had been gone. I wasn't the type of guy to usually freak out, but I had. It was pathetic. So much so that I hadn't even thought about texting her to find out where she was until Aaliyah had told me to.

When Payton had informed me that she was with my father at his hotel having breakfast, I'd damn near torn the hotel room to shreds in a fit of rage that caught me by surprise.

Payton was alone with Conrad and Lauren.

Why, I had no fucking clue. But I knew I had to get her away from them. She wasn't safe with either of them.

Now, as I walked through the huge casino, looking for the restaurant she had mentioned, I was seething. I knew something was up. I should've known my father would do something underhanded, but honestly, I hadn't expected this. If he had actually taken her aside and instructed her to meet him without my knowing, then there were plenty of reasons for me to be worried.

He clearly didn't want me there.

Well, guess where I was?

Fuck that old bastard.

When I reached the restaurant, I ignored the hostess who tried to stop me as I entered, waving her off as I stepped into the dining area. I stopped long enough to glance around, and that was when I noticed Payton sitting at a table in the back. She was studying her coffee cup, looking like she'd rather be anywhere but there.

I took a deep breath and tried to calm down. I was just planning to politely interrupt their breakfast to see if she was ready to go.

That had been the plan.

Until I saw Trevor Yates sitting beside her.

Much too close for my peace of mind.

I approached the table as quietly as I could, unable to keep my hands from balling into fists at my side.

"What the fuck is going on?" I asked as soon as I got their attention.

Okay, so much for trying to politely interrupt. My voice was louder than I intended, and it would appear I had caught the attention of most of the people sitting around them as well.

Fucking awesome.

Payton's eyes flared, and her mouth dropped open as she looked up at me.

Yeah, I probably sounded like a raging lunatic, but she had no fucking clue just what type of crazy bastard she was sitting next to at the moment. Nor did she have any idea that the man sitting across from her was likely the devil himself.

"Conrad, I thought we agreed he wouldn't be here," Lauren said softly, her hand gripping my father's arm tightly. "Your assistant should be more than capable of handling her job without him babysitting her."

Lauren's condescending tone did nothing for my mood.

"Capable?" I asked, glaring at her. "She's quite capable, I agree. But" — I shot a look at Trevor — "when you introduce her to pieces of shit like him, I have to wonder just what your angle is."

"Sebastian, shut your mouth," Lauren snapped, her icy stare boring into me.

"Excuse me, *ma'am*," I said, tacking the last part on because I knew how much she hated that. "I didn't realize they allowed trash in this place. Had I known, I would've kept a better eye on my girlfriend."

"Girlfriend?" Conrad shot to his feet, his gaze darting back and forth between me and Payton.

Oh, come on. He really didn't know? I seriously doubted that.

I slid my gaze over to Payton.

Shit.

The look on her face reflected her embarrassment, and I knew without a doubt that I was acting like a jackass, but I couldn't help it. If she knew what I knew, she would have stayed far away from every single person at that table.

"Please tell me you haven't allowed him to brainwash you," Lauren said softly, speaking directly to Payton. "He's…" Lauren glanced down at the table, but she didn't finish her sentence.

Payton's hand came up over her mouth as though she was shocked by my stepmother's words. I wasn't. She'd said plenty worse than that before.

"I should've warned you, Payton," Conrad told her.

I was tempted to punch him in the face.

"Warned me about what?" Payton asked, her eyes moving back and forth between Conrad and Lauren. Although it was clear she was upset with me for barging in like that, I could tell she was pissed at Conrad and Lauren as well. I could deal with her anger. What I wouldn't be able to deal with was her believing these manipulative assholes.

"Conrad's son… He's" — Lauren lowered her voice and continued — "unstable."

Unstable? Seriously? That was all she had?

"Damn right I'm unstable," I ground out through clenched teeth. "But at least I'm not a…" I bit my tongue before the words slipped out. This wasn't the place to get into it. Not with a restaurant full of people who were now focused on us. "Are you ready to go?" I asked Payton, keeping a tight grip on my temper.

"If I'd known he would act like this, I would've warned you just how messed up he really is," Lauren added. "He's always been the jealous type. And he doesn't like Trevor very much."

Very much was an understatement. I despised the lying, scheming, disgusting bastard. But I didn't say as much. It wouldn't have helped the situation.

Payton got to her feet, glaring at Conrad and then turning her murderous scowl on me.

Yeah, I'd gone and fucked up royally. I knew it. I deserved her wrath.

"If you'll excuse me," Payton said softly.

I reached for her arm, but she sidestepped me, looking at me as though I'd lost my mind.

"This isn't over," I warned my stepmother before I turned to follow Payton.

I managed to take two steps, but I was pulled up short when Conrad grabbed my arm. "That's where you're wrong. This *is* over. It's been over for a long time, Sebastian."

I jerked away from him, but I managed to keep my mouth shut.

Barely.

By the time I caught up with Payton, she was stepping outside in front of the hotel. She asked the valet to get her a cab, but I waved him off.

"Payton." When I reached for her again, she spun around to face me, her eyes wild, her chin trembling.

"How dare you?" she hissed, tears forming in her eyes. "How dare you embarrass me like that? Did you forget that I work for that man? He signs my paycheck. If he tells me to join him for breakfast, that is what I'm paid to do. I was handling the situation just fine."

"You don't have a fucking clue what was going on there," I growled, keeping my tone low.

"No, you're the one who doesn't have a clue, Sebastian," she retorted.

"Come on, I'll take you back to the hotel."

"Don't touch me," she snapped when I tried to take her hand. "Get the hell away from me, Sebastian."

I swallowed hard, staring at her. I knew what she was thinking. In retrospect, I could have handled that much better than I had. Then again, I could have handled it much worse. She just didn't know me well enough to see how much I'd just held back.

"I'm going to the show. I'll wait for Conrad to arrive. And I'll see you at the hotel tonight. Until then" — she paused, taking a deep breath — "I don't want to see you."

"Payton." She knocked the wind out of me with that statement, but I did my best not to let my pain show. If she only knew. If she had any idea what type of people she was dealing with.

Working for Conrad was one thing. She was surrounded by other people at the office. People who would notice if something were awry. But to be alone with him in a place where people thought he was a god because of his money... If she only knew, she would understand why, from now on, I would make it my mission in life to ensure he didn't get near her again.

He would not interfere. I would not lose her, too.

I watched as Payton turned and walked away, getting into a cab that was waiting at the curb.

Thrusting my hands through my hair, I tried to control the rage that had my insides vibrating. The chaos was back. The noise louder than ever. And as I glanced back at the hotel where my father was, I was tempted to go back inside and do what I should have done a long time ago.

But I didn't.

For whatever reason, I managed to rein myself in, stepping back from the edge.

It wasn't fucking easy.

Chapter Nineteen

Payton

How I made it through the day, I had no idea. After the debacle at breakfast with Sebastian showing up and acting like a lunatic, I'd been hard-pressed to find a hole to crawl into.

Unfortunately, dealing with Mr. Trovato all day had been the equivalent of handing a three-year-old a box of crayons and convincing him not to draw on the wall. No matter how many times I told him that I didn't want to talk about Sebastian and that I was fine, he tried to find a way to bring him up anyway.

Luckily, Mr. Trovato had been scheduled to give a seminar, which gave me a little over an hour of free time. After ensuring he had his notes and water, I had ventured off on my own. I was happy to find that Lauren hadn't attended the show, and when I mentioned that to Conrad, he informed me that she wouldn't be present for the remaining two days, either. If anything positive could be said about the whole thing, it was that I didn't have to deal with her.

I'd had more than my fill of her that morning, thank you very much.

The woman scared me. Between her icy stare and her apparent dislike of Sebastian, I honestly didn't care if I ever saw her again.

After Conrad's seminar was over, we visited the Trovato, Inc. booth, and now he was sitting in on a panel of people talking about performance engines. Since I knew I had at least an hour to wait, I slipped into the hallway to call Chloe. I needed to talk to her.

"Hey, hooker. How's it going in Vegas?" Chloe's cheerful greeting instantly put a smile on my face.

"It's goin'," I replied, lowering myself to a padded bench against the wall and setting my purse down in front of me.

"Uh-oh. What's the matter?"

She knew me all too well.

Figuring she was going to get it out of me eventually, I blurted out what had happened that morning.

"Your first fight as a couple. How cute," Chloe replied sweetly after I had spilled my guts.

"Seriously? That's what you took away from all that?"

"What did you want me to say?"

"Oh, I don't know. How about telling me that I did the right thing? Or that I wasn't wrong to storm out on him."

Chloe's lack of response made my stomach hurt.

"Breathe, Payton."

Breathe? I wasn't sure that was possible. I suddenly had the vision that I would go back to the hotel to find Sebastian not there. All day, even though I was incredibly pissed at him, I'd longed to see his face, to feel his arms around me. I wanted him to assure me that everything was going to be fine. That what had happened that morning was stupid.

"Payton, you really need to talk to him about his father," Chloe said, pulling me back to the moment.

"I don't know what to ask him," I admitted truthfully. "I mean, seriously. I don't know how to deal with that sort of family drama."

"Oh, that's right. Sometimes I forget that you grew up in a bubble full of roses and dandelions."

I snorted, picturing myself in a bubble filled with flowers. "That's not what I meant, and you know it."

"Something's not right between those two, Payton. Based on what you've told me, that's not just family drama. Sebastian's intense, I'll give you that. There's something dark about him, but I can't imagine he'd pull a stunt like that without a good reason."

That was exactly what I'd been thinking that morning when I'd climbed into a cab and made my way back to the MGM Grand for the convention. "You should've seen him, Chloe. He was so pissed."

"Because you went to breakfast without him?"

"No. That wasn't it. He was angry because I was there with Conrad. And the look he gave Lauren's nephew, I'm surprised the guy didn't go up in smoke."

"Why was he there, anyway?" Chloe asked.

"Who? Trevor?"

"Yeah."

"Hell if I know. I never figured that part out. Trevor mentioned that he was considering a career change and that was why Conrad had invited him to breakfast."

"In Vegas?" Chloe's exasperation mirrored my own.

"I know, right? He doesn't live here."

"So why's he there?"

"No idea. But he gave me the creeps, to tell you the truth."

"Maybe Sebastian was right to interrupt."

"Chloe, I was having breakfast with my boss. I get that Conrad is his father, but that wasn't a casual conversation."

"Or it wasn't supposed to be," Chloe added. "It sure sounds casual to me."

She was right. It was surprisingly casual, especially considering I'd never had to attend anything like that with Conrad before.

"Maybe Trevor just showed up out of the blue. And Lauren invited him."

"I don't think so." Based on the way they'd spoken, I seriously doubted that was just a chance encounter.

I heard a muffled conversation in the background and realized that Chloe was talking to someone. She uncovered the phone and I heard her say, "I'll be right with you. One sec. Hey, Payton. I have to go. My next appointment's here."

"Okay."

"Call me later, okay? I want to make sure you're all right."

"I will," I promised and disconnected the call, staring down at my phone.

Checking the time, I realized I still had a good half hour before Conrad was out of his meeting, so I decided to call Aaron. Talking to Chloe had eased my mind, but she hadn't given me any suggestions on what I should do next, and I was still out of sorts.

I dialed Aaron's number and hit talk, glancing down the wide hallway while I waited for him to answer.

"What's up, buttercup?" he greeted, his tone as cheerful as Chloe's had been. "How's Sin City?"

"I wish I was home," I told him.

"Oh, hell. What's wrong, doll?"

Again, I launched right into my story from that morning. Telling Aaron about Conrad insisting I attend breakfast and that Sebastian wasn't supposed to know. Then about being introduced to Trevor, Lauren's creepy nephew. Aaron didn't speak until I had run through the whole thing, ending my story with me getting in a cab and leaving Sebastian behind on the sidewalk.

"Did you ask Sebastian why he did that?"

"No," I answered. "When would I have had time to do that?"

"Oh, I don't know. You've got time to call me, don't you?"

Good point.

"I haven't talked to him. I needed time to cool off."

"Listen to me, Payton. I'm gonna tell you something you don't want to hear."

I grumbled into the phone and Aaron laughed.

"Seriously. You like this guy, right?"

"No, Aaron," I said, taking a deep breath. "I love him."

Aaron was silent for a moment, and I knew what he was thinking. I'd never loved a man before. Even my college boyfriend had just been a guy I was dating. He had been my first and only sexual partner, but I'd still never loved him. I had liked him a lot, but my heart had never been fully invested.

"Well, then. That makes what I have to say all the more important."

"Spit it out, would ya?" I said, exasperated.

"Doll, if this guy means something to you, and clearly he does, you need to get his side of the story. I get that you were embarrassed, but that honestly doesn't sound like something Sebastian would do just for the hell of it."

Aaron was right. Sebastian didn't seem like the kind of guy who tried to draw attention to himself. That came naturally, but in the time that I'd known him, he hadn't once tried to be the center of attention.

"And Payton … you're an adult now. Adults have conversations. They talk things out. You might think you know him, but I guarantee you don't know everything."

"Trust me, that's the last thing I think. He's got secrets. I know that."

"Then find out what they are. Find out how you can help him. That's part of being in love. It's not all about the good times and the incredible sex."

I snorted, my face burning although Aaron couldn't see me. "I never said anything about sex."

"Honey, I've known you long enough. I know a satisfied look when I see one."

"Shut up," I insisted, giggling and letting my hair drape over my face to hide my flaming cheeks.

"Seriously, doll," Aaron said, all amusement gone. "Talk to him. The guy's a ticking time bomb, and from what it sounds like, you're the only one who can cut the wires before it's too late."

I sighed. That wasn't exactly what I wanted to hear, but I understood what Aaron was telling me. I did need to talk to Sebastian. I needed to know what I was really dealing with. We weren't going to be able to move forward until we got that part figured out.

"Thanks, Aaron. I needed that."

"I know you did. Call me later and tell me how it went. Oh, and doll?"

"Yeah?"

"Have a little fun while you're there."

"I'll try."

With that, I hung up the phone and looked up to see people piling out of the conference room. Apparently the session was over. I grabbed my purse and jumped to my feet, going toward the fray rather than away from it. When I found Conrad, he was talking to someone so I stood back so as not to interrupt.

He glanced around and must've noticed me because he held up one finger to the guy, a signal for him to hold on before he came over to me. "Why don't you go back to the hotel early today? Maybe you and Aaliyah can go out and see the sights."

I was confused as to why Mr. Trovato was brushing me off, but I wasn't about to argue. If he didn't need me anymore, I was certainly content to get out of there. "Yes, sir."

Without so much as a good-bye — not that I had really expected one — Conrad returned to the man, and they went in the opposite direction, picking up their conversation as they walked.

I was grateful that Conrad had let me off the hook for the rest of the day, although I wasn't sure why he had made such a huge turnaround. Just yesterday, he'd been an ogre, and today he was actually being almost nice. The logical answer would be that he knew I was embarrassed about what had happened at breakfast. But for some reason, I didn't think that was the answer, either.

As I walked toward the main entrance where I'd come in, I considered that. I figured Conrad's strange attitude shift had to do with the fact that Sebastian wasn't hanging around. As happy as I was that Conrad wasn't treating me like a lackey, it pissed me off that he treated Sebastian like shit. And worse, that he seemed happier when Sebastian wasn't around.

What kind of father treated his own son like that?

"Payton."

I turned at the sound of my name to see Sebastian leaning against a wall just outside the hotel. The moment I saw him, I stopped walking.

He looked … so damn sexy.

Apparently a couple of other women thought so, too, because they were standing a few feet away, talking and smiling in his direction. Sebastian seemed oblivious, and that made my heart do a slow somersault in my chest. To think that those women wanted him and he was mine made some of my confusion over what had happened that morning dissipate.

I was pretty sure that Sebastian was the sexiest man on the entire planet. And standing there so casually, he looked … hot.

How that was possible when he also looked like he hadn't slept in two days, I wasn't sure. The black sweater he donned, even though it wasn't tight, showed off his incredible physique and offset his golden eyes, making them glow. The distressed jeans showcased his muscular thighs, and the heavy black boots on his feet gave him a dangerous edge. There was still that intensity about him. His hands were thrust in his pockets, his mouth a firm, thin line, and he seemed uncertain as to whether he should approach me.

The moment our eyes met, I felt the tension drain from him. The muscles in his shoulders and neck were still rigid, but there was a second of relief that registered on his ruggedly handsome face.

"Please ride with me," he said, his voice gruff, his tone pleading as he moved closer to where I had stopped. He seemed hesitant, and I instantly remembered the argument from that morning. And then I remembered what Aaron had told me. My best friend was right. We were adults, and the only way we would get through this was if we talked it out. Running wasn't the right answer, and staying away from him was an impossibility, no matter how upset I was.

So, when Sebastian reached for my hand, his callused fingers wrapping around mine, I knew that there was no way I could even pretend to resist him, so I nodded my head.

And followed him to the car.

Chapter Twenty

Sebastian

For the first time since Payton had walked away from me that morning, I felt a sense of peace overcome me. The noise in my head had settled to a dull roar. It wouldn't be completely quiet until she and I had a chance to talk, but for now, this was considerably better than the hell I had endured all day.

After she'd gotten into a cab that morning, I had gotten in another and followed her. In fact, that was what I'd done the entire day. For every minute she'd spent inside the hotel at the SEMA show, I had been right there with her. Today, I'd managed to stay out of sight on purpose. I wasn't there to stalk her. I was there to protect her. I doubt she would've understood that, but my conscience wouldn't allow me to leave her alone with Conrad. Not even for a minute.

And the instant she'd stepped outside, her eyes meeting mine, I had finally released the breath I'd been holding the entire day.

The limo ride to the hotel was silent, and we made our way up to our hotel room without speaking. But holding her hand was enough for me. Touching her was a comfort that I'd never known before.

But the silence ended the instant we stepped inside the hotel room.

"Shut up, Leif! Just shut the hell up!" Aaliyah screamed from the top of the stairs.

I followed her gaze to see Leif standing at the bottom looking both angry and dejected. Apparently, the two of them hadn't worked out their issues.

"What's going on?" Payton whispered to me, squeezing my hand tightly.

"Lover's quarrel," I muttered.

"Fuck you, Sebastian," Aaliyah squealed. "He is not my lover. I wouldn't touch him with a ten-foot pole!"

Okay, then. I should've been happy about my sister's declaration, but honestly, my head hurt, and I just wanted to spend a little time alone with Payton. I had intended to order room service and lock ourselves in the hotel room for the night, hoping for a chance to talk to Payton about my outburst that morning, but it didn't look like my night was going to go according to plan.

"What happened?" Payton asked, her voice louder. She obviously wasn't talking to me. If she was, I certainly didn't have an answer for her.

"*He* happened!" Aaliyah yelled, stabbing the air in Leif's direction before stomping to her room and slamming the door.

Leif thrust his hand through his hair and turned to face me and Payton. "I'm sorry, man."

"What did you do?" Payton clearly wasn't giving up on her questions, so I resigned myself to getting these two to talk things out.

Leif dropped onto the couch and let his head fall back on the cushion, staring up at the twenty-foot-tall ceiling. "I'm a dumbass."

"Obviously."

Payton elbowed me for my comment and then released my hand. I couldn't say I was happy about that, but I followed her anyway. She took a seat on the sofa next to Leif, watching him intently.

"Y'all stayed out all night last night, didn't you?"

"Yeah," Leif replied. "It started out as a good night."

"And then…" Payton obviously wanted him to fill in the blank.

"And then we went to a strip club."

"Oh." Payton's wide eyes made me smile, but I remained behind her so she couldn't see. Strip clubs didn't do it for me, but Leif had been known to drag me to one a time or ten. Even without Leif's explanation, I could pretty well guess what had happened.

"We both had a little too much to drink," Leif admitted. "One of the strippers kept bugging me, so I paid for a lap dance. Don't ask me why." Leif glanced over at me.

I could tell he was pained by whatever had happened, but part of me figured he deserved it, so I said, "Because you're a dumbass. You said so yourself."

"Yeah, thanks." Leif clearly didn't find my statement amusing.

Seriously, the guy had taken my twenty-one-year-old sister to a strip club in Vegas. Couldn't say that was a great selection for a first date, but what did I know.

"I'm gonna go check on her," Payton said, looking back at me over her shoulder.

I nodded, knowing that I wouldn't be able to stop her.

When I heard Aaliyah invite her into her room, I turned to Leif. "You're a fucking idiot, you know that?"

"Yep. First rate. I got that."

"Why'd you take her there?" I asked, curious.

"It was *her* idea," Leif retorted, his tone defensive. "I suggested that we go check out the casinos downtown. We got down there, had a few drinks, and all of a sudden, she wanted to go to a strip club. I'm serious, man. It really was her idea. Said she wanted to do something she'd never done before."

"And you're the idiot who took her?"

"Yeah." Leif sighed. "She was fine until the lap dance. When it was over, she stormed out. I followed her, made her get in a cab back to the hotel. She refused to come back here, so we went to the Golden Nugget."

"And then what?" I asked. "You argued about a stripper?"

Leif's gaze met mine, and I saw something I'd never seen before. Pain.

"What happened?" I questioned again, needing the details.

"She'll kill me if I tell you," Leif answered.

"I'll kill you if you don't," I ground out, keeping my voice low.

"Damn it," Leif exclaimed, thrusting his hands through his already messy hair. He leaned forward and put his elbows on his knees, head hanging low. "I kissed her."

"Please, God, tell me that a kiss didn't lead to this bullshit."

"No, it was what came after."

I was ready to punch him in the mouth. Ready to launch my fist right at him if he told me he'd tried to sleep with my sister.

But Leif surprised the shit out of me with his next statement.

"Aaliyah told me she was a virgin," Leif began quietly. "Said she had always wanted me. That she wanted me to be her first. She offered no strings attached." Leif looked over at me, his eyes sad. "When I told her I wanted strings, that I couldn't see us ever hooking up unless we were dating, she got pissed. I think she took it as a rejection."

I didn't know what to do with that information. I suddenly found myself not quite so angry, but I had no idea why. I knew Leif had liked Aaliyah for a long time. And I knew she liked him. That was apparent.

But Leif wanted a relationship with my sister? That was … interesting.

"Did you apologize?" I asked him.

"A million times. She won't listen to me. And when she does, she ends up screaming at the top of her lungs."

Definitely sounded like something Aaliyah would do.

She had the spoiled-little-rich-girl thing down pat. On top of that, she had a volatile temper like I did. But unlike me, she wasn't able to channel her anger. I had mastered that art a long time ago. Mainly because if I hadn't, I would've ended up in jail for killing someone by the time I was twenty.

Payton appeared at the top of the stairs, her gaze meeting mine. When she headed toward our bedroom, I stood, turning back to Leif. "You need to talk to her. And if she won't listen, you're gonna have to do something to get her attention."

Leif nodded, but he didn't say anything. I waited a moment but then headed upstairs, finding Payton in the bedroom with the door open.

"Can we go get something to eat?" she asked as soon as I stepped into the room, her voice soft. "I'm starving."

"Of course." Reaching for her hands, I slid my thumbs over her knuckles as I watched her.

The thought of kissing her had plagued my mind most of the day, but I hadn't intended to do so until I had a chance to explain myself. Fortunately for me, Payton took that decision away from me when she stepped closer, her hands squeezing mine before she released them and cupped my jaw, pulling me down to her.

Her lips were soft against mine, her hands cool against my face. "I love you," she whispered, and I swear to God, I nearly cried.

I hadn't cried once since the day my mother had died. Not one single time. But right then and there, with Payton whispering the sweetest words I would ever hear, the only words I *needed* to hear, I was tempted to cry like a fucking baby. I'd spent the day unraveling, scared that I'd fucked up beyond repair, but yet, she told me that she loved me.

"I love you, too," I whispered back, my voice rough with emotion. "I'm sorry about this morning."

Payton's finger covered my lips, stopping me from continuing. "Let's go get some food. Give those two a few minutes to work things out, and then we can come back and talk."

I nodded. I'd go anywhere she wanted me to. Just as long as I could have her with me, I didn't care where that was, either. I think I proved that when we made it to the food court and my beautiful girlfriend decided she wanted McDonald's for dinner.

So, while we shared French fries and ate Big Macs, I listened to Payton tell me what her day had entailed after she'd left me at the hotel. Although I'd been witness to it because I had stayed close, I still loved to listen to her talk. She could probably read me the dictionary and I'd hang on every single word. When she was finished, she went on to tell me about her conversation with Aaliyah.

Only then did I say more than two words. "So, my sister's pissed because Leif doesn't like her?"

"That's her version," Payton advised.

"But he does like her," I told her, confused.

"I know that. And you know that, but she clearly doesn't know that."

"How could she not? The guy's a slobbering idiot when she's around."

"I think that's part of it. When she tries to talk to him, I think he's too nervous to open up to her."

That was surprising as hell. Considering when I was around Leif, he never shut the hell up.

"Aaliyah said they went to a strip club," Payton told me, her eyes roaming my face as though she expected a certain reaction from me.

"That's what Leif said."

"She said it was her idea," Payton added.

"He told me that, too. He also told me that he turned her down when she wanted to sleep with him. According to him, he wants a relationship before that happens."

"Wow. She kinda left that part out," Payton said softly, her gaze remaining glued to the table.

I noticed that Payton was no longer eating, choosing rather to stir a French fry around on the tray before tossing it down and grabbing a napkin to wipe her hands. I leaned back in my chair and studied her. There was something on her mind, and I knew it had nothing to do with the argument between Aaliyah and Leif. I was expecting her to mention what had happened that morning, and I was fully prepared to defend myself, but what came out of her mouth shocked the shit out of me.

"Aaliyah told me that you're moving."

Well, hell.

That definitely wasn't what I'd expected her to say. Shit, I hadn't expected Leif to say anything to anyone, but I should've seen it coming. A close second behind Toby, Leif couldn't keep his mouth shut, either.

Before I could respond, Payton said, "I think that's really what started their argument last night. Aaliyah's really upset."

"Damn it," I muttered, leaning forward and resting my forearms on the table and clasping my hands together in front of me. When I'd told Leif that I needed him to hold off on moving in until I finalized the sale on my new house, I hadn't considered the fact that he would blab to my sister. I had wanted to be the one to tell her. I knew she wasn't going to be happy with me, but I knew that if I remained that close to my father for much longer, the shit was really going to hit the fan.

Unfortunately, I hadn't considered the repercussions of telling Leif before I talked to Aaliyah.

"Is it true? Are you moving?"

"Are you finished?" I know it sounded like I was avoiding her question, but honestly, I just wanted to find someplace else to have the conversation.

Payton nodded.

"You want some coffee?" I asked, nodding my head toward the coffee shop behind her.

"Sure," she answered.

I grabbed the tray of food and carried it to the trash can, dumping the contents before taking her hand and heading to the coffee shop. I ordered two large coffees, and after Payton doctored hers to her liking with cream and sugar, I snagged her hand again and led her through the casino and out the front doors.

The sun was setting, and the temperature was comfortable, so I opted to sit on a stone wall. After hoisting myself up, I pulled Payton back against me so she stood between my legs. I was at the perfect height to rest my chin on the top of her head, so I placed my coffee down beside me so I could wrap my arms around her.

"I bought a house," I began. "I've been debating on taking the leap for a while. I guess you could say that recent events have inspired me to move forward."

"Me?" she asked, a measure of surprise in her tone.

"Yeah." I knew it was the perfect opportunity to tell her what I'd nearly blurted out a few days ago, but I couldn't bring myself to do it. Not there. Not in a city she was unfamiliar with. I didn't want her to freak out and run away, so I came up with something on the fly. "Living at the guesthouse has its perks, but it's time for me to get out of there. I need somewhere that I don't have to worry about Conrad barging in. He owns the place, and as long as I live there, he's got me under his thumb."

Payton nodded as though she understood, her hand resting over the top of mine. "Where are you moving to?"

"North," I told her.

"North of where you are now? Or north of Austin?" she asked.

"Both," I answered, chuckling. "But definitely north of Austin."

Payton turned her head to look up at me. "Closer to me?"

I studied her for a moment, wondering what I should say. Or rather, how she would respond to it. "Yeah. Closer to you."

She surprised me when she smiled and nodded her head. I wasn't sure if that was because she liked the idea of me being closer or if it was because she thought I'd gone crazy.

But I guess a smile was a smile. And since she wasn't running far and fast, I had to consider that a win.

For now.

Chapter Twenty-One

Payton

Sebastian and I stood outside the hotel talking, mostly about his new house, until the sun sank behind the mountains and the air cooled considerably. When I began to shiver, we came back inside the casino, but we bypassed all of the games and headed up to the room. We walked in to find Leif and Aaliyah sitting on the couch watching television.

Aaliyah looked content, although her eyes were puffy, proof that she'd been crying. But she certainly looked more at ease than she had earlier. She had changed into yoga pants and a T-shirt, her blond hair pulled up in a ponytail, her youthful face scrubbed free of makeup. There was an empty tray on the table in front of them, which I assumed had contained their dinner at some point.

"No more yelling?" Sebastian asked when he closed and locked the door behind us.

"Not at the moment," Aaliyah answered, her eyes moving to Sebastian. I instantly recognized the concern on her pretty face and knew she was probably wanting to talk to her brother. After all, Leif had dropped a huge bomb on her that really hadn't been his place to divulge. Then again, maybe he hadn't realized that she didn't already know.

"I'm gonna go take a bath," I whispered to Sebastian, hoping he would take the hint. His eyes raked over my face before meeting mine again, as though he were trying to understand what I was telling him. When I noticed his brows furrowing, as though he expected the worst, I leaned in and pressed my lips to his gently. "When you're done talking to your sister, maybe you can join me."

He nodded, a small smile curling the very corners of his lips, and I made my way to the stairs without looking back.

Once inside the bedroom, I closed the door and sat on the edge of the bed. I was exhausted. After last night, staying up so late, and then having to rush out of bed that morning only to traipse around the huge trade show, I was ready to just pass out.

Figuring I had a few minutes before Sebastian arrived, I kicked off my shoes and pulled back the blankets on the bed. If I just closed my eyes for a few minutes, that was all I needed, and then when Sebastian returned, we'd get in the bath together.

"Morning." Sebastian's deep voice greeted me as soon as my eyes opened. I instantly closed them, trying to block out the blinding light that was filling the room.

"Did I seriously sleep all night?" I asked, my voice raspy from sleep. I curled into Sebastian, placing my hand on his flat stomach as he pulled the blanket up over my shoulder.

"That you did. You're quite the party animal in Vegas," he told me, kissing the top of my head.

"I was only supposed to close my eyes. I was waiting for you to join me before I got in the bath," I explained.

"You were out cold when I came up here. I couldn't bear to wake you."

"Thank you for letting me sleep." As I lay snuggled in his arms, I forced my eyes open slowly, acclimating to the bright morning sun. "How'd it go with Aaliyah?"

"Better than I thought it would," he said, wrapping his arm more tightly around me. "She understands. She was just pissed that I hadn't told her."

"I don't blame her." I was a little hurt that he hadn't told me and that I'd had to hear it from Aaliyah. But we had only been together for a short time, so I didn't let it bother me.

"Want to get some breakfast before you have to go to the show?" Sebastian asked after several moments of silence.

"I need to shower first," I told him, not wanting to get out of bed. I was too warm, too comfortable being with him, and I didn't want the day to intrude on that moment. If I had a say in the matter, I'd stay in bed with him all day and say to hell with the show.

But then I'd probably lose my job, which would only start a domino effect of shitty things to happen. So, instead of wasting away the day in the comfort of Sebastian's arms, I pushed up onto my arm and looked at him. "Want to join me?"

The sexy, crooked grin that he gifted me with made my body come alive instantly. I knew that look. It was a look that said I was about to be in over my head.

Two minutes later, Sebastian proved to me just how true that statement was. The water had barely warmed before he was backing me into the huge glass enclosure that took up half of the bathroom. Before the door even closed behind him, his hands were on me, roaming, searching, teasing. When his mouth joined the mix, I had to bite my lip to keep from crying out. His lips started their journey on mine, then moved slowly down my neck, then to my breasts, where he tormented me with delicious lashes of his tongue against my nipples. And just when I thought I couldn't handle any more, he stood, pressing me against the wall.

"I need to be inside you," he murmured against my lips.
I nodded, desperate for him to do just that.

Twining his fingers with mine, Sebastian lifted my hands above my head, holding me there. While the warm water cascaded over us both, he slid inside me slowly. I moaned, my head thumping against the tile as I let the sensations overwhelm me.

"So tight," Sebastian groaned, his hips pressing into mine as he filled me completely.

As he thrust deep inside me, his teeth nibbling my neck, I closed my eyes, savoring the moment. I loved being with him, loved to feel him touching me, kissing me. The sexy words he said only launched me higher. I wasn't sure I would ever get enough of him. The way he moved, the way he thrust into me. He was so powerful yet controlled. As though he was holding back, not wanting to hurt me. For a brief moment, I wondered what it would be like if he ever unleashed the beast and took me with all the intensity I knew was built up inside him.

I doubted I would survive it.

"Angel," Sebastian growled as he moved up to my lips, his tongue thrusting into my mouth as he drove himself deeper. The need for oxygen made it difficult to kiss him, and when he pulled back, he said, "I need you to come for me, Angel."

I was close. So close, but I didn't want it to end, didn't want him to stop. But when he clasped my wrists with one hand and lowered his other between our bodies to tease my clit, I couldn't hold back.

He quickened his pace, and I lifted my leg, placing my foot on the small ledge, offering him easier access. He pounded into me, his hand gripping my wrists tightly, his thumb grazing my clit, his mouth sealed to mine as he kissed me with a ferocity I hadn't known before.

"Come for me, Angel," he demanded, his tone harsh, his control clearly slipping.

"Oh, God, Sebastian. It feels so good."

"Come for me," he pleaded, his thumb pressing against my clit, and then suddenly there were tiny colorful lights flashing behind my closed eyelids as my body shattered. Sebastian groaned, his mouth moving back down to my neck as he continued to thrust into me. "Payton. Angel." A deep growl erupted from his chest, and he stilled as he climaxed, his body pulsing deep inside me.

Twenty minutes later, after Sebastian thoroughly washed my hair and my body, then I returned the favor, we climbed out of the shower. While I put on my makeup, he dressed and went downstairs, leaving me to my thoughts.

Standing in front of the bathroom mirror, I brushed the long strands of my damp hair, allowing the hot air to slowly dry it, remembering the incident from yesterday morning. Then I remembered my conversation with Aaron. I knew that Sebastian and I needed to talk. Last night, I'd thought he was going to open up to me when we were outside, but he hadn't. But I had to wonder whether our avoidance of the conversation was more my fault or his. Or if both of us were just sidestepping the issue. Considering Sebastian was moving out of the house he lived in on his father's property and into one of his own, I knew that things were about to come to a head between them. I couldn't help but wonder what that meant for me.

Would my involvement with Sebastian cost me my job?

Did I really care?

Or would my job cost me Sebastian?

Those were things I'd never imagined I would have to worry about, but now that was all I could think about.

I loved Sebastian. That wasn't just my hormones talking, either. I loved everything about him from his quick, easy smile, his sexy laugh, to that deep-rooted vulnerability that most people never saw. I especially loved his intensity, although it scared me a little. Aaron was right, Sebastian was a ticking time bomb, and he was set to go off at any moment.

So the bigger question was … how did I stop that from happening? And if I couldn't, how did I pick up the pieces in the aftermath?

Chapter Twenty-Two

Payton

Saturday morning

"Oh, my God! I'm so glad you're home!" Chloe squealed when I walked through the front door of my apartment on Saturday morning.

Luckily I managed to brace myself before she threw her arms around my neck and squeezed me tightly or I would've landed flat on my ass. Sebastian was right behind me, carrying my luggage despite my previous argument that I could manage on my own. When he joined us inside, he offered a lopsided grin before continuing on to my bedroom, returning empty-handed and leaning against the wall.

The last two days had been relatively uneventful — thank God. I'd worked with Conrad during the day, and Sebastian had insisted on staying close. On Thursday evening, we'd gone to dinner with Aaliyah and Leif again, and I was glad to see they were back on speaking terms. The one thing I did notice was that Leif was keeping his distance. I think that whatever had happened between them had hurt Leif, but I don't know what exactly that was. Neither of them were very forthcoming with all the details from their night out. I could tell that the two of them hadn't told us the complete story, but I didn't press them on the issue, either.

Then after I'd spent most of the day at the SEMA show on Friday, the four of us had ended up going to a night club last night, where we'd danced and drunk until the early-morning hours. It was then that Sebastian had informed me that he had changed my flight so we could go home together. I was surprised to find out that Aaliyah had gone back on the same flight with her parents and Leif had gone with us.

I had initially been relieved that he'd taken the initiative to keep me with him, but then it hit me just what he'd done. It was a possessive move, one that I really needed to think about more. I was a grown woman; it would've made sense for him to ask me first, but he hadn't. Having endured more than my fair share of arguments for one trip, I had opted to keep my opinion to myself until I had time to process it more.

We were all fairly quiet for most of the flight, and I had opted to sleep for the majority of the three hours it had taken for us to get back to Austin.

At the airport, Leif had gone his separate way while Sebastian had driven me home in his Camaro, which he had parked at the airport. Now that I was standing in my apartment, I suddenly wished that our trip had lasted a little longer, because I didn't want Sebastian to leave. But I could tell by the way that he was watching me that he was about to do just that.

Shaking off the needy thoughts, I tried to focus on Chloe, who was grinning at us both.

"Did y'all have fun?" Chloe asked, stepping back and looking at the two of us with a curious smirk on her lips. "Y'all didn't go and get married while you were there, did you?"

I choked, my face heating at least several thousand degrees. Married? Good grief. The woman lived to torment me.

"Not yet," Sebastian stated seriously, and I spun around to face him only to be met with a sexy grin. "I need to get home. I've got something to take care of today."

I nodded, accepting the fact that our trip was officially over even though I didn't want it to be. Sure, I was happy to not have to go in to work for a couple of days, but spending time with Sebastian had become second nature while we had been away. So much so that I feared having to spend the night alone in my bed.

Yep, the neediness was out in full force, and truthfully, it was beginning to piss me off.

"I want to take you to dinner tonight," Chloe insisted. "You can tell me all about the trip."

I glanced back at my friend, forcing a smile. I knew what she was doing. She was going to make sure I didn't sit at home tonight and pine after this man.

And I loved her for it, because if it weren't for her offer, I would probably close myself off in my bedroom and relive every minute of the trip until I made myself absolutely crazy.

"Sounds like a plan," I said with forced enthusiasm.

"Walk me out?" Sebastian asked, pushing off the wall and taking my hand.

I nodded and followed him down the stairs. We stopped beside his car, and he leaned against the door, turning to face me. I was having a hard time looking at him because I didn't want him to see the disappointment on my face.

Sebastian tipped my chin up with his fingers, forcing me to look him in the eye. "I'm glad I got to spend the last few days with you."

For some reason, that statement felt an awful lot like a good-bye, and I was suddenly scared that he was saying something more. "Me, too," I whispered, barely able to get the words out.

"I'm gonna be busy for a few days, but I want to see you, Payton."

I nodded my head, unsure what I was supposed to say. It was probably pretty apparent that I was missing him already.

"If you don't hear from me for a couple of days, please don't worry."

Okay, so now I was really worried. How could he seriously tell me that and expect me to do the opposite? "Why..." I couldn't get the question out, so I swallowed around the lump in my throat and tried again. "Why wouldn't I hear from you?"

"I've got something to take care of."

My mind drifted to everything I knew about Sebastian and everything I'd heard, but I couldn't come up with any reason that he would practically fall off the face of the earth for a couple of days. Maybe this was his way of dumping me. Had things really gone that badly? I tried to recall the last few days, but the memories evaded me. Maybe he thought that after a couple of days I would forget all about him.

I swallowed hard, pissed at myself for being so damn insecure. I wasn't the clingy type, never had been, yet here I was trying to come up with every worst-case scenario I could. And that made me mad.

"No worries," I told him, hoping I sounded more confident than I felt. "You've got things to do and so do I."

"Payton," Sebastian drew out my name slowly, his arms banding around me and pulling me to him. He pressed his mouth to my ear. "You're not getting rid of me, Angel. Not that easily."

I didn't want to get rid of him, but I didn't tell him that. Once I turned into the desperate, insecure girlfriend, we were both going to regret it. So, I simply hugged him back, pressing my forehead to his chest. "I'll be here, Sebastian."

He pulled back, but only far enough so that he could press his mouth to mine. He tasted of mint and sexy male. For whatever reason, probably because my mind was already considering this our final good-bye, I kissed him, wrapping my arms around his neck and devouring him. If this was going to be my last kiss, I was damn sure going to make it worth my while.

By the time we pulled back, we were both panting for air. I avoided his gaze but wrapped my arms around him tightly just because I didn't want to let him go.

"I'll call you tonight," he told me, but I got the impression he was saying what he thought I wanted to hear. After all, he had just informed me that I might not hear from him for a couple of days.

But I didn't call him on it. I couldn't. Hell, I could barely swallow, so I knew the words weren't coming easily.

By the time I closed my bedroom door, sealing myself in my room so that I could have a few minutes to myself, I was gasping for air.

Something was wrong. Really, really wrong. I could feel it.

And whatever it was, Sebastian didn't want me to know.

Chapter Twenty-Three

Sebastian

If anyone ever mistook me for some sort of fucking martyr, they didn't know me all that well. What I'd just done wasn't because I thought leaving Payton was what was best for her. In fact, if that were the case, then by God, I would do wrong by her for the rest of our lives because this … this was just temporary.

Although, I could tell by the look in her eye that she thought I wasn't coming back.

She was so very wrong.

Driving away from Payton was harder than it looked, and it damn sure hadn't been what I wanted to do, but it was something that had to be done. For now. I hadn't lied to her when I told her I had something to do.

Last night, after we'd come back to the hotel room, after I'd stripped Payton and made love to her for a solid hour, I had lain awake for hours, my thoughts refusing to slow long enough for me to sleep until just before dawn. Then when I finally had succumbed to sleep, I'd been plagued by that damn dream again — the one where the race ended with my Camaro engulfed in flames.

That — the race — was the real reason I had walked away from Payton. The woman calmed me to the point of distraction, and if I had any plans of walking away from the race in one piece, I needed the chaos to return.

Considering I'd dreamed about Payton and she had practically materialized right there in my world, I was getting a little paranoid about the dream. Dying in a fiery blast wasn't something that I had on my agenda these days. A couple of weeks ago ... well, maybe I hadn't cared all that much then. But I certainly did now.

I wasn't leaving Payton.

And as much as I wanted to spend every waking moment with her, I knew that I needed to get my head on straight. When I'd barged into that restaurant and lost it, I'd taken a turn that I hadn't expected. Keeping my suspicions to myself was one thing. Until I had hard-core proof of what I feared, I knew that any accusations against my father would likely end up with me in a mental institution.

The bastard was a powerful man. More powerful than I usually gave him credit for.

So, after leaving Payton at her apartment, I drove toward the highway, pulling off in the gas station to make a couple of phone calls. The first one was to my realtor buddy, Jim. I asked him to meet me at the new house so I could take care of a couple of things. He informed me that everything was good to go and they'd scheduled an inspection for next week. Provided everything came back good, I was hoping to be moving in less than a month.

The next call I made was to Toby, telling him to meet me at my house in an hour. I had already asked Leif to stop by before we'd gone our separate ways at the airport. I wanted to talk to them both before the race. My chat with Toby was quick, and once he agreed to meet, I pulled out of the parking lot and headed north on the interstate.

Less than ten minutes later, I was pulling through the automatic gate that surrounded the house that I was in the process of buying. While I waited for Jim to arrive, I climbed out of the car and walked around the perimeter of the house. It was empty, had been for a few months, which had worked in my favor.

After checking things out, mostly to pass the time, I sat on the front steps, staring out at the acres of land that surrounded the property. That was what I was most excited about, I think. The idea of building a track and a shop of my own and starting the next phase of my life was getting to me. It was high time I did something that didn't include being underneath Conrad Trovato's thumb all the damn time.

Getting away from him was imperative, but more important, I had to figure out what to do about the other thing. The secret that I'd buried for so long. The suspicion I had that was transforming into fear.

I didn't scare easily, but ever since I'd met Payton, ever since she'd become the most important thing to me, I knew that I had a hell of a lot to lose. And I couldn't risk it.

"Hey, Sebastian." Jim's optimistic voice pulled me from my thoughts, and I got to my feet, reaching out and shaking his hand.

Jim let me in the house, and I spent a good twenty minutes looking things over, trying to figure out just what I needed. Moving out of Conrad's house, I would have nothing. Nothing more than my personal effects, which meant I had to make some big purchases.

I was ready.

"Hey, Jim," I called, my voice echoing in the empty house.

If I said the house was modest, I'd be lying. It wasn't as ostentatious as my father's, but it was impressive. Six-thousand square feet with an additional twenty-five-hundred-square-foot indoor pool wasn't something to balk at. But in my defense, the house was a steal. And the fact that it sat on over two hundred acres, surrounded by nothing but farmland, only made it all the more desirable, in my opinion.

"What's up?" Jim asked as he met me in the entryway.

"I need some measurements. Can you get the appraisal expedited? Or find someone who can get them to me ASAP?"

"I'll see what I can do."

I slapped Jim on the back. "Thanks. Oh, and let's get this done in two weeks. Not a minute longer."

I walked out of the house with Jim staring at me as though I'd lost my mind. Maybe I had. But after spending the last few days with Payton, I knew it was time to do what needed to be done.

And when that moment came, all hell was going to break loose.

I needed somewhere to go by that time, and this was going to be it.

Half an hour later, I was pulling through the gates at my father's estate. I continued past the main house, wondering when would be a good time to inform Conrad that I was done.

And by done, I wasn't just talking about moving out and living on my own.

I was fucking done.

Done with him period.

Considering I really was the reason Trovato, Inc. had been continuing to grow over the last few years, I didn't expect my father to take the news lightly. Although he'd threatened to replace me numerous times, even he knew that wasn't a smart move.

Now he wasn't going to have a choice.

But the bigger issue was trying to figure out how to get Payton away from him before he retaliated against me, which I was certain he would do.

Granted, just because I quit working for him didn't necessarily mean that she would have to. But then again, she didn't know my secret. And I needed to be prepared for the worst once I finally told her.

There had been more than one opportunity to talk to her while we'd been in Vegas, but I had chickened out. That was all there was to it. I didn't know how to tell her. Didn't know how she was going to react. And I damn sure didn't want her trying to get away from me in a city that she wasn't familiar with. In a place she didn't have anyone who would be there to take care of her if it came down to it.

So, I'd held back. Again.

Just like I was holding back now.

I made my way to the guesthouse, pulling into the garage. I wasn't surprised to see Toby's car parked in the driveway, nor was I shocked to see him sitting on the couch in my garage when I pulled in.

He stood and greeted me, a wide grin plastered on his face.

"It's about fucking time," Toby said, coming toward me when I climbed out of the car.

"Did you miss me, you fucking pansy?" I asked, smiling as I said it.

"Fuck no," he retorted. A lie if I'd ever heard one. "I hadn't even realized you were gone."

"Liar." I popped the trunk to retrieve my luggage, pulling out the bag and setting it on the floor.

"How's Payton?" Toby asked, following me as I headed into the house.

"Good."

"Y'all have a good time?"

"Yeah." I wasn't going to go into the fight we'd had just yet. It was bad enough that Leif knew all the gory details because he'd been at the hotel when Aaliyah had mentioned it the next day.

"Have you told your old man that you're movin' out?" Toby asked as he made a beeline for the refrigerator, pulling out two bottles of water and tossing one to me after I shrugged out of my jacket and threw it over the chair.

"Not yet." It was inevitable, but I knew my father. He was on the verge of cutting me off. Or at least he was on the verge of believing that was even a possibility. He didn't give me enough credit, though. I'd long ago taken the necessary precautions to ensure he couldn't hurt me. At least not financially.

When you blackmailed someone into handing over a significant amount of money in order to keep silent, you did what was necessary to ensure the bastard couldn't start backtracking. And I'd done that the second I'd turned eighteen.

While my father believed he was still in control of my money, I knew better. I mean, seriously, I wasn't a fucking idiot. Sure, there was a little money left in the account he knew about, but the majority of it had been moved long ago. For the last seven years, I'd allowed him to believe that I was shitty at managing my money, choosing to blow it on stupid shit, but that had never been the case. Had he looked hard enough, he would've noticed, but Conrad didn't expect much from me.

"Hey, we still on for tonight?" Toby asked, hopping up onto the counter and staring at me.

"Yep." I knew he was talking about the race. Toby was the guy I depended on to get me into the races. Due to his money situation, he rarely went in when so much was at stake, but he was always right there with me. "You didn't say anything to Chloe, did you?"

"Nope. I'm not a complete dumbass."

"Really?" I asked, pretending to be shocked by the news.

"Fuck off. And I didn't do it for you, asshole. I don't want her anywhere around that shit."

"Can't blame you there," I told him, twisting off the cap on the water bottle and tossing it into the trash can as I leaned against the counter.

A street race was significantly different than a race on private property like we'd done last weekend. There was always the risk of getting caught, which so far hadn't happened. But as the races became more popular, there were considerably more folks who came out to watch, and with crowds like what we'd seen the last few times, it was definitely getting risky.

"Leif wants in," Toby told me, his expression serious.

"Why?" I asked. If history repeated itself, Leif wasn't going to win, which meant he'd be out two grand. Although I'd give it back to him if he asked, I knew he wouldn't.

"It's not always about the money," Toby told me.

"Well, no shit." For me, it wasn't ever about the money. It was about the rush I got from driving. It was about quieting the noise in my head. Until Payton, it had been the only thing that worked.

"Does Payton know?"

I shook my head, downing the rest of my water and tossing the bottle into the recycle bin. "Nope. And I don't plan to tell her, either."

"She's gonna be pissed."

I doubted it. I wasn't one for lying, by omission or otherwise, but in this instance, I didn't want Payton to know. And what she didn't know wouldn't hurt her.

If only that were true with all my secrets.

Chapter Twenty-Four

Payton

Saturday night

"He did *what?*" Chloe's voice was loud, causing several heads to turn and look at us.

I leaned forward and told her to keep it down, knowing it wouldn't do much good.

Aaron was sitting beside Chloe, staring at me as though I'd lost my mind.

"Why would he do that?" Chloe asked, her loud whisper not doing anything to quiet her down.

"I don't know," I admitted. "I guess he really likes her."

I had just finished telling them the story about the incident between Aaliyah and Leif. Apparently, what happened in Vegas really didn't stay in Vegas. Not when I was the one who had to put up with Chloe's constant pestering. I'd finally given in and told her the story. It was that or rehash the fight I'd had with Sebastian, something that Chloe was incredibly curious about.

Although I'd told her everything on the phone, she had insisted that I retell the story just to make sure I hadn't left out any details. When I'd refused, the conversation had moved on to Leif. And before I knew it, I was airing all their dirty laundry.

"Don't you dare say anything to Toby," I warned Chloe.

She smirked, sipping her water. "I'll try."

"So what ever happened with that guy Trevor?" Aaron asked.

Obviously he didn't have a problem remembering the details like Chloe had.

"Did you see him again?" Aaron asked, cocking an eyebrow as he waited for me to answer.

I knew I wasn't going to get out of it. Aaron was just as pushy as Chloe when he wanted to be. "Nope. Not once."

"Do you find that weird at all?" Chloe asked.

Well, of course I did, but I didn't get to answer because Aaron spoke up.

"It sounds like your boss was trying to set you up."

"With *Trevor*?" I asked, stunned. "Why would he do that?"

"To keep you away from Sebastian, maybe," he retorted.

"Like that would ever happen. That dude was seriously creepy," I told him. "But you know, he did mention that he was considering a career change. If he meant that he would be working for Conrad, why wouldn't he be at the trade show?"

"Maybe that was a lie," Chloe said, picking at her noodles with her fork.

"Why would he lie?" I asked.

"Maybe it was a set-up. Maybe they were hoping you'd tell Sebastian." My eyebrows rose as I waited for her to elaborate. I wasn't understanding what she was trying to tell me.

"You said the guy was a mechanic. It's possible that Conrad wanted you to tell Sebastian so he thought he was being replaced."

"Well, that's just stupid," I blurted.

Aaron laughed. "No one said the guy was right in his head. I mean, seriously, he keeps his own kid a secret."

"That's just weird," Chloe added. "Why would he do that?"

"I don't think he wanted people to know that he got an underage girl pregnant," I told them truthfully, taking a sip of my raspberry tea.

"Yeah, well, that's super creepy," Chloe stated, shivering.

I knew what she was feeling. It was disgusting to think that Conrad had been with a teenage girl. More so that he had gotten her pregnant and then turned his back on her.

Knowing that they would continue to grill me about Sebastian if I let them, I decided to change the subject. "So what did you and Toby do while I was gone?"

"Not much," Chloe answered, her smile once again brightening her face.

"Not much, my ass," Aaron inserted. "The guy practically lives at our apartment."

"Shut up. You're just jealous."

"Maybe," Aaron admitted truthfully, laughing.

"Are you gonna see Garrett again?" I asked, watching him closely.

"It's a possibility."

"How much of a possibility?" When Aaron didn't share details, I knew he was hiding something.

"He's coming into town next weekend."

"Have you talked to him?" Chloe asked, turning her head to look at Aaron.

"Every night."

Wow. A lot had happened in the few days I'd been gone. It appeared that Toby and Chloe were officially a couple and possibly on the verge of living together, and it looked like Aaron might've found someone to help him move on from Mark.

I was happy for them both, but even sharing that with them didn't help ease the unsettling feeling I'd had since Sebastian had driven away from me that morning.

"Where's Toby tonight?" I asked Chloe. I was being nosey, more for my own benefit than anything else.

"He didn't say," she admitted. "I told him I was taking you to dinner and that we were gonna veg on the couch and watch cheesy chick flicks all night. He said he'd talk to me tomorrow."

"Aren't they doing that street race tonight?" Aaron asked, pushing his plate away and reaching for his water glass.

I dropped my fork, the metal clattering against the glass plate. "Oh, shit."

Chloe's eyes widened as she realized the same thing I had.

Sebastian was racing tonight. That was why he'd left me that morning. That was what he'd had to do.

Son of a bitch.

"What time is it at?" Aaron asked, as though he weren't the one who had just told us what we had obviously forgotten.

Chloe snagged her cell phone from her purse and stabbed the screen several times. She was watching me as she put the phone to her ear. "Where are you?" she said by way of greeting a few seconds later.

I wanted to hear what was being said on the other end of the phone, but with the noise in the restaurant, I couldn't make out even a hint of the conversation.

"Toby Brindle," Chloe said through gritted teeth, "don't you *dare* lie to me."

There was another pause while Chloe listened to him speak.

"Shit. Okay."

Another pause and I was hanging on by my fingernails.

Thankfully, the waitress showed up and handed me the check. I slapped my credit card down and turned my attention back to Chloe.

"Oh, bullshit, Toby. Don't you even think about it. If you don't tell me where you're at, don't expect to see me naked ever again."

I laughed — I couldn't help myself. If that wasn't a threat, I didn't know what was.

Chloe was studying my face as she listened, her eyes widening slightly. I was holding my breath, anxious for her to tell me what he said.

"We're on our way." Chloe disconnected the call and stared back at me. "You might wanna tell that waitress to hurry the hell up. We've got twenty minutes before the race starts."

Aaron whistled through his fingers, waving his hand and getting the waitress's attention. I was too worried to be embarrassed. But it worked. The waitress arrived, took the credit card, and five minutes later, we were piling into Aaron's Honda while Chloe rattled off the directions.

Aaron was one of those cautious drivers who always obeyed the speed limit, never forgot to use his blinker, and even slowed down to a near crawl before he made a turn. I was feeling sorry for him now although I was more on Chloe's side than his at the moment. She was yelling at him, telling him to go faster, when to change lanes, where to turn. She was the absolute worst backseat driver. What made it worse was that she was riding shotgun. I was hanging on for dear life in the backseat while Aaron alternated between random acceleration and jerky turns. Chloe was clearly turning him into a basket case.

When we arrived at our destination, I looked around, trying to figure out just what was going on. If this was the place, then it was abandoned. Maybe that was part of the plan, what with an illegal street race and all, but when I say abandoned, I mean there wasn't a single soul anywhere. Not another car, not a single person walking down the street.

"Do you think he gave you the wrong place?" Aaron asked, his hands white-knuckling the steering wheel.

"He better not have," Chloe snapped, digging her phone out of her purse.

Before she got the chance to dial, I heard the rumble of an engine and turned to look out the back window, noticing there were at least fifteen sets of headlights coming toward us.

Toby's '69 Camaro pulled up alongside Aaron's car, stopping suddenly before Toby jumped out. He flung open Chloe's door and squatted down in front of her. He looked pissed.

"I really don't want you here," he told her firmly.

"Well, screw you," she argued. "I have every right to be here."

And just like that, Toby seemed to calm down. He reached up and cupped Chloe's face while Aaron and I stared at them.

"Seriously, baby. This is too dangerous. If the cops show up, I don't want to have to worry about you."

Okay, so their lovey-dovey stuff might've been sweet, but I really didn't care to sit by and watch it. Throwing open my door, I stepped out, the glare of headlights shining on me.

"Payton, get back in the car," Toby demanded, standing up straight and stepping in front of me.

"Where's Sebastian?" I asked, furious that Sebastian hadn't told me about the race. Well, technically I'd known about it, but he had deliberately left off that detail when he'd told me he had things to do.

"He's on his way," Toby replied. "He's gonna freak when he finds you here."

"Why?"

"Because he doesn't want you to get in trouble. Or worse, hurt."

I glared at Toby, not liking his answer. Mainly because it made sense. "I want to see him."

"Payton," Toby said softly, touching my arm. "Think about this for a minute. Do you really think he'll be able to concentrate if he knows you're here?"

Damn it. Why did Toby have to be so freaking logical?

Before I could argue, a big guy with a shaved head and a tattoo on his scalp walked up to Toby. "We gonna do this shit tonight, Brindle?"

"Yeah," Toby growled. "In a fucking minute."

The big guy's beady eyes narrowed on Toby, and I instinctively took a step back, closer to the car. "You might wanna send the children home to their mommies. Wouldn't want 'em to get hurt."

"Shut the fuck up, Rebel."

Rebel? Seriously?

"Honey, if you'd like to ride along, I'll be more than happy to let you climb aboard." The guy was talking to me, grabbing his crotch as he spoke.

"Fuck you," I snapped, both angry and disgusted.

I was watching the big guy named Rebel, and the next thing I knew, he was stumbling after Toby slammed into him, shoving him hard. "Stay the fuck away from them, Rebel. You hear me?"

Now, I had only known Toby for a little while. And usually, he was a sweet, laid-back charmer who was always smiling, usually making some sort of witty comment. I could not for the life of me place that guy with the guy I saw now.

"You wanna piece of me, asshole?" Rebel yelled at Toby, moving toward him and slamming his chest into Toby's.

I thought Toby was going to hit him, but he didn't. Instead, he simply said two words, and it was as though the night swallowed everyone. "She's Sebastian's."

It was eerily silent, aside from the hum of car engines, until Aaron yelled at me from inside the car. "Get in the car, Payton."

I took one step back and bumped into the car door.

"Now get in your fucking car, Rebel. He'll be here in a minute. Hey, Joey! Get 'em on the starting line." After Toby was finished yelling his instructions, he turned to face me. "Payton, I'm serious. You need to get out of here. At the least, please don't let Sebastian see you."

I nodded. It wasn't like I could argue with him. He'd just nearly beaten up a guy for the way he'd talked to me. I was a little freaked out and a lot scared, so I crawled into the car and closed the door gently, still watching Toby as he walked over to Chloe.

He leaned into the car, twisting so he could see Aaron. "If you wanna watch the race, go back there. They'll be coming around that turn." Toby pointed behind us. "But don't you fucking dare let Sebastian see her." Then Toby kissed Chloe quickly and whispered something into her ear. She didn't say anything, just nodded her head. Then Toby took a step back and closed the door.

Aaron put the car in gear and drove toward a row of buildings that made up the main street of the small downtown area. I had no idea what town we were in, but I knew it wasn't Austin. There was no way they'd be able to race on Austin roads and not get caught. But maybe, in this little nowhere town, they wouldn't get caught.

"What did he say?" Aaron asked Chloe.

She peered over her shoulder at me and then back to Aaron. "He said he has a bad feeling about this. And he wants me to keep my cell phone on me."

My heart sank right then and there. I twisted in my seat to stare out the back window, watching the headlights move as everyone got into place. I didn't see Sebastian's Camaro yet, but I knew he'd be there.

Which was what worried me the most.

Chapter Twenty-Five

Sebastian

After Leif called and told me he had something he needed to take care of and he'd see me at the race, Toby had decided to head out, too. I handed over my cash for the race, and for a brief instant, I considered telling him about my dream. At the last second, I opted to keep it to myself. I figured he would try to talk me out of the race, and I couldn't back out, even if I wanted to.

When the house was quiet, I decided to spend a couple of hours working out, trying to get my focus. I blared the music, beat the heavy bag until I was drenched in sweat and my fists hurt. And when I had damn near exhausted myself, I took a shower.

The only good thing about the afternoon was that somehow I'd managed to get my head on straight. That was the reason I was behind the wheel of the Ferrari and my Camaro was sitting in the garage with my keys in the seat. I had backed it out once but immediately pulled it back in. I just couldn't let go of the dream, and since it was always my Camaro that I was in when the thing exploded, I figured I might be able to avoid the inevitable if I left the damn thing at home.

It was dark when I left the house. I took the toll road because I knew it would have the least amount of traffic and I could hit speeds in excess of one-twenty, which I did almost the entire way. But once I exited the highway, I dialed it down a notch as I made my way through the small town that had clearly closed up early on a Saturday night.

I found Toby standing outside with a handful of others. They were all placing bets and ribbing one another about who was going to win. I tuned them out, making my way over to Toby. "Have you heard from Leif?"

"He's on his way," Toby said quickly, turning to take money from some other guy.

I spun in a circle, looking at the crowd that had gathered. If we didn't get this show on the road, some backwoods deputy was going to likely come upon us soon. I turned back to Toby. "Let's get a move on. I've got shit to do."

Toby nodded. "You heard the man."

With that, I made my way to my car, slid inside, and grasped the steering wheel with both hands, inhaling deep and slowly exhaling. I waited for the others to take their places on the line. There were only three cars that pulled forward; the others scattered in all directions. And I waited before pulling up on the far right.

Toby stopped at each of the cars, chatting with the drivers, probably getting their money as well. I turned up the radio, refusing to get lost in my own thoughts. Just a little while longer and then I'd be home free. I had even decided that once the race was over, I was going to stop at Payton's. I needed to see her. Screw giving her a few days. I wasn't going to last that long without seeing her beautiful smile.

I nodded my head when Toby passed by my car, his fist pounding once on the roof before he moved on. The engines were beginning to rev, and I glanced down the line, noticing that there were still only three.

Some chick I didn't know, dressed in a halter top and jeans although it was cold as shit, came strutting out in front of the cars, waving what looked like a scarf.

I waited, the car in neutral, one foot on the break, the other tapping the gas. I kept my eyes trained on the girl, waiting for her to give the go-ahead. I was beginning the countdown in my head when I saw another set of headlights brighten the street in front of us. I glanced down to see a black car at the end, pulling into the line. Before I could try and get a better look at the driver, the girl in front of us waved her hand up slowly and then slapped the air when her arm came down.

And the race was on.

Although I wasn't used to racing the Ferrari, the damn thing had some serious power, and I used every bit of driving skill I had, pulling out in front and staying there. Accelerating down the straights, double-clutching around the turns, weaving in and out, keeping the others behind me. I glanced in my rearview a couple of times, trying to keep up with the location of the other drivers while still keeping my eye on what was in front of me. I noticed the black car gaining, sliding in front of the yellow Mustang, easing beside the electric-blue Charger, so I did a few evasive maneuvers. It wasn't until a particularly sharp turn that I got a better look at the black car.

My car.

My fucking Camaro.

And Leif was at the wheel.

Shit.

Fuck.

Damn.

My heart skipped a beat as I peered out in front of me, noticing our location. The route had been mapped out ahead, and we were closing in on the finish, only a couple more turns to go. I swallowed hard, my eyes flipping back and forth between the night in front of me and the car in my mirror.

Fucking shit.

It took everything in me to keep my thoughts on the finish line, but as we got closer, that became harder and harder. One more turn and then it would be straight the rest of the way. The corner was sharper than I'd anticipated, but I managed to keep the car under control, kicking up the RPMs and downshifting through the turn.

I had just made it through when I looked in the mirror to see the others coming around the same turn and then it happened…

My world went into slow motion when the electric-blue Charger clipped the back end of my Camaro, sending Leif into a spin and then…

"Fuck! No!"

Oh, God. No.

No. No. No.

My worst nightmare had just come true, but worse than seeing my car go up in flames was watching my best fucking friend in my Camaro rolling multiple times before coming to an abrupt stop on its roof.

I slammed my foot on the brake, turned the wheel, and damn near collided with the fucking Charger coming head on. Fuck the race. I had to get to Leif.

I could see the Camaro, upside down on the side of the road, flames licking from under the hood. I was pretty sure my heart stopped beating. Everything else I did from that moment forward just happened; I don't recall making any conscious decisions.

I just did.

I just moved.

And somehow, I just breathed.

"Leif!" I screamed his name at the top of my lungs after launching myself from my car, running full out to where he was.

I could see him. His face was a bloody mess, his head cocked to the side, his arm twisted at an odd angle, and he was dangling upside down, the seat belt holding him in place. I could smell gasoline, knew it was leaking.

The flames were what scared me.

"Fuck! Leif, wake up, man!"

I had to get him out. The nitrous was going to ignite.

"Leif! Wake the fuck up!"

I managed to wrench the door open a little, cramming myself between the door and the body of the car, using all of my strength to force it open. When I managed to get my shoulders through, I reached around Leif, trying to find the seat belt buckle. I fumbled a few times, unable to get it unlatched.

"Bastian," Leif murmured, his usually booming voice so damn weak.

"I'm here, man. Gonna get you out."

I carried on an unintelligible conversation for the next few seconds, until finally I managed to free the fucking seat belt. Not moving Leif wasn't an option. I only prayed that I wasn't doing more damage, but as the flames grew, I knew that nothing was going to matter if I didn't get him away from the fucking car.

I heard the squeal of brakes and then Toby's voice.

The next thing I knew, we had pulled Leif free of the car, dragging him back toward the street.

"It's gonna blow," Toby yelled as we continued backward, trying to put as much distance between us and the car as we could.

There was a roar, and then the world exploded around us, knocking me off my feet. I flew through the air, hit the pavement hard, slamming my shoulder, and then my head met the concrete. I was momentarily stunned, but I managed to make my brain work, rolling over onto my back. Forcing my eyes open, I could see Leif lying a few feet from me, Toby crawling back toward us.

The sirens in the distance were getting louder.

"Wake up, Leif! Hey, Sebastian? You okay?" Toby's voice sounded strange to me, like I was in a tunnel.

"I'm good," I replied, unsure if he could hear me.

My head was pounding, there was blood running down into my eye, and my shoulder throbbed like a motherfucker. I must've hit my head, but I didn't remember it. Fighting the blackness that teased the edges of my vision, I crawled over to Leif and Toby. Just those few feet took everything out of me.

I could hear people moving around us, more cars, more doors slamming.

My body gave out beside Leif, but I managed to stay conscious, watching Toby's face as he checked Leif out. It was bad. I knew that much. The sirens were loud now, the noise making my head throb.

"Sebastian! Sebastian!"

I knew that voice.

My angel.

Payton.

I tried to look around, but I could hardly move my head. It felt like someone was stabbing me in the face with an ice pick.

"Sebastian! Oh, God. Oh, my God."

When Payton appeared in front of me, I nearly broke. I reached for her, and then she was in my arms, tentatively touching me, brushing my hair aside, looking at my face.

"The ambulance is on the way," she informed me.

I shook my head. "Leif." I didn't need an ambulance. Leif did. He was the one who was hurt. I would be fine. I just needed to close my eyes for a little while.

"Is he okay?" Payton asked, and I opened my eyes enough to see that she was talking to Toby.

"Leif," I muttered again.

"He's right here," she told me, glancing past me and then back down at my face. "Hang on, Sebastian. Please hang on."

"Angel," I whispered, squeezing her hand, "I love you."

She whispered that she loved me, too, and then the world went black.

From the author

I really hope you enjoyed Unraveling, the second book in the Unhinged series. Book 3 will be out in October 2014!

Payton and Sebastian's story came to me one day when my husband and I were driving in the car. I mentioned a plot idea to him and he told me to go for it. After writing the first book in a matter of days, I asked my daughter to read it. Her excitement and eagerness for more encouraged me to publish their story.

You can stay up to date on the additional books in this series by going to my website:
www.NicoleEdwardsAuthor.com.

If you don't want to miss any release dates, sign up for my newsletter and you'll receive the information right to your inbox on release day.

About Nicole Edwards

New York Times and *USA Today* bestselling author Nicole Edwards lives in Austin, Texas with her husband, their three kids, and four rambunctious dogs. When she's not writing about sexy alpha males, Nicole can often be found with her Kindle in hand or making an attempt to keep the dogs happy. You can find her hanging out on Facebook and interacting with her readers - even when she's supposed to be writing.

Website: www.NicoleEdwardsAuthor.com
Facebook: www.facebook.com/Author.Nicole.Edwards
Twitter: www.twitter.com/NicoleEAuthor

Nicole also writes contemporary/new adult romance as Timberlyn Scott.

More by Nicole Edwards

The Alluring Indulgence Series
Kaleb
Zane
Travis
Holidays with the Walker Brothers
Ethan
Braydon
Sawyer
Brendon

The Club Destiny Series
Conviction
Temptation
Addicted
Seduction
Infatuation
Captivated
Devotion
Perception
Entrusted

The Dead Heat Ranch Series
Boots Optional
Betting on Grace

The Devil's Bend Series
Chasing Dreams
Vanishing Dreams

Standalone Novels
A Million Tiny Pieces

Writing as Timberlyn Scott
Unhinged
Unraveling
Chaos

Made in the USA
San Bernardino, CA
08 February 2018